Dedication

To my lovely wife Elisabeth,
Also my children & their partners,
And my grandchildren.

Acknowledgements

I thank all who have listened to and sometimes commented on extracts from my stories. My wife Elisabeth continues to be a perceptive listener, who comments usefully. My family have been supportive – e.g. Barbara Seale encouraging her dad after seeing an early draft. Local writers – Formby Writers and the U3A group – have listened helpfully to brief extracts.

I'm especially grateful to my son Colin Douglas who has guided me through the publishing process.

On creative writing, my learning has been facilitated via The Writers' Bureau, Lancaster University, the Writers' Workshop and NAWG conferences, and (with Formby Writers) Gabrielle Rollinson, Margy Mcshane and Professor Helen Newall.

TABLE of CONTENTS

Tales with Twists

An Anthology of Stories

By Bill Douglas

An assortment of short pieces – mystery, romance, drama, fantasy, suspense, with many a twist. Conflict and reconciliation, despair, hope and love all abound, amid the interplay of relationships

Preface

I wrote these tales over a number of years and edited them to create this anthology. Listed alphabetically, the assortment is varied and without a common theme. In the pages are mystery, romance, suspense, psychological action, family drama, interplay of relationships, danger, grief, living with challenges – and occasional glimpses of humour. Two can be classed as this 'real world' fantasy – told from the respective viewpoints of Jenny the ghost and Esme the cow.

Of the twenty-one pieces, nineteen are short stories. These vary in length, from the two 50-word mini-sagas to over 3,000 words, with most around 1,500-2,000. The time-span in most is short – though in *Illegal Immigrant* and *Life Sentence* the important back stories cover many years. In *Rocky Road* the tale is set out in a one-act play with three scenes. *Hearing Voices* is a reflective article with poetic fiction in the middle.

My love of short stories began in early youth – with O. Henry, Damon Runyan, Somerset Maugham, WW Jacobs, Neil Munro and PG Wodehouse. I did not then try writing stories, and over the decades my reading interests veered towards classic novels then textbooks relevant to work. On retiring, I came back to short stories, and thought I'd try writing a few. I gradually realised that creative writing called for a different approach to tackling articles, and sought much-needed tuition. I was then drawn to writing a historical novel*, before preparing this selection for publishing.

I enjoyed writing these tales. I hope you'll enjoy reading them.
Bill Douglas
April 2018

* *'Mad Worlds: A Tale of Despair and Hope in 1950s England'*
Troubador 2014

1. Alison

Though it was six years ago, I remember clearly that fateful sunny afternoon. I was stepping along lightly, homeward bound without the slightest sense of foreboding. I shouldn't have stopped.

But I did – and gaped as she strolled by. "Alison?" I half shouted, uncertain. It had been a long time.

She stopped and turned to face me. The dark eyes fixed on me, then sparkled as her face transformed with that cheeky smile. "Dammit, Bob!"

With sudden re-kindled passion, I gave her a hug.

"Nearly didn't see you," she said.

"Time for a coffee?" I asked, conscious of pedestrians manoeuvring round us.

She glanced at her watch. "Okay – let's." A frown creased her face. "Can't be long, though."

"I know just the place – only a jiffy from here. Follow me."

She nodded. "Hold my hand. Don't want to lose you."

As we weaved along the crowded pavement to a table inside Alberto's cafe, I felt a surge of excitement as her hand pressed into mine. I squeezed back tightly.

Seated, we opened simultaneously. "Where –?" We both stopped and looked at each other.

She laughed. "Just like old times."

Puzzling. "How come?"

"We always wanted to talk, and neither of us would listen." Her expression changed – looked wistful.

I reflected a moment. This hurt. "But I was going to ask where the heck you disappeared to all that time ago?" Just over ten years, in fact.

Her lips tightened, and she drew a sleeve across her eyes. "You never really loved me," she charged.

"Alison, I did. I was so damn busy at work. Couldn't you see?"

"No." She fished in her handbag and produced a mobile. "Here, I'd love a photo," she said. Flattered, I duly posed.

I eyed her appreciatively. "You haven't changed, Alison." True. Her face looked more drawn, but her beauty hadn't faded – rather, matured – and she had the same enchanting smile and super figure.

She gazed at me. "You're balder and you stoop. But you're still the same old Bob."

We sat in silence while I digested this unsolicited testimony. Another sign she hadn't changed. The finesse of a Rottweiler!

I noticed she was looking past me. I turned to follow her gaze and caught a glimpse of a man in a grey suit standing looking our way.

"Bob – I must go."

I swung back to face her. "But, the coffee…"

She rose suddenly, bent forward and kissed me lightly on the forehead. The aroma was mildly intoxicating – she hadn't changed from that alluring perfume. "Sorry," she breathed.

"Hey – how can I contact..?" But she was away, tripping off into the crowd, not looking back. I stood up, trying in vain to follow her progress. I couldn't see the man in the grey suit either.

I sat down again and hunched over the table for a minute, feeling a bit stunned and thinking of what might have been. We'd been an item – really close.

But one evening ten years ago I'd got back to find a note saying we were finished – no explanation – and asking me not to try finding her. I'd gone over and over in my mind, searching for a reason, contacted our mutual friends.

As the waiter approached, I waved him away.

I picked up my briefcase and continued my journey homeward. The love of my life had again vanished.

* * *

It was three days later. Lyn and I had just finished our evening meal and were in the kitchen as the coffee percolated – when the bell rang.

Janie, our 8-year-old, rushed to answer then shouted "Dad!" Something strained about her cry made me respond immediately.

"Hello?" I queried, as I brushed past Janie to confront the two strangers on our doorstep.

"Robert Gunn?" asked the woman.

"Who wants to know?" Any mild trepidation was more than offset by the three glasses of wine. I squared up boldly to the pair.

The woman held up an ID card. "Police," she said. "Inspector Jones and" – she inclined her head toward her male companion – "Sergeant Robson. May we come in, sir?"

I scrutinised the card. Looked genuine. "Yes… and yes I am Robert Gunn."

What on earth could this be about? I showed our visitors into the front room then took a puzzled-looking Janie by the hand through to see Lyn.

"The police – no idea why," I responded to Lyn's questioning look. We persuaded Janie to stay in the lounge watching television and went through to meet our visitors.

"I'm Mrs. Gunn. What's this about?" asked Lyn.

"Well, it's your husband we really want to see," said the Inspector. She looked at me. "Is it all right with you, Mr. Gunn, if your wife remains?"

"Of course!" I exploded. "This is *our* house, and" – I glanced at Lyn, whose cheeks had reddened – "I've done nothing wrong."

"Right, over to you Sarge." The Inspector nodded to her colleague.

"I'll come to the point, Mr. Gunn." The Sergeant coughed. "We believe you know a woman by the name of Alison James."

"No – never heard of her." Obviously mistaken identity.

"Do you mean *the* Alison James?" Lyn asked quietly.

"Yes, Mrs. Gunn," said the Inspector. "She's been something of a celebrity. Wrote for television and had a regular column in *Women's Universe*."

"Oh, I definitely don't know her." I stood up, ready to show our visitors out.

"And her maiden name was Holt," said the Inspector, not moving.

I needed to sit down. "I used to know an Alison Holt – about ten years ago."

"Did you know her very well, sir?" asked the Sergeant.

"Oh, fairly well – yes – at that time." I was aware of Lyn gazing at me and felt myself blushing. "But it was long ago."

"We have evidence you were with her last Friday afternoon, sir." The Sergeant's tone had a nasty edge.

"Last Friday – hmm." I paused, stomach churning, thoughts racing. Yes it was Friday. But how did they know and why were they here? I hadn't told Lyn about meeting Alison – though I had mentioned her previously as a girl I went out with long ago. I could feel sweat begin to dampen my face. Damn – that wine. "Evidence? What sort of evidence?"

"Photographic, sir – and CCTV. You seemed friendly."

"What *is* this about?" demanded Lyn.

The Sergeant hesitated. Then the Inspector came in with the thunderbolt that just about wrecked my life. She said quietly, "Your husband, Mrs. Gunn, may be the last person to have seen Alison James before her disappearance."

I could sense all eyes boring into me. The sweat was now running.

"Is my husband a suspect?" demanded Lyn.

"No – not at this point at least. He's just helping with our enquiries," answered the Inspector.

The D.I. went on to explain that Alison had been reported missing by her husband early Saturday morning. She'd been due home the previous evening. The police had contacted her conference hotel, established she'd paid her bill, and found her car still parked there.

The police hadn't rushed into enquiries – despite her TV producer husband's pressure – as they thought it might be a case of having a 'night on the town' or 'a fling with a conference guest'. But when by Saturday evening she hadn't shown up, they searched the car, found her travel bag and handbag in the boot, then launched a 'missing person' inquiry.

By the Sunday evening, having spotted my mugshot on the mobile, spoken with Alberto's manager and accessed CCTV recordings, they decided to pay me a visit.

* * *

Six years on, my recollection of that time is vivid – and I've set out the tale of these encounters as accurately as I can.

Alison and her husband were so renowned (to the masses – though not to me) that her disappearance had plenty mileage for the popular press. 'ALISON MURDER?' was one tabloid's banner headline. While the article contained only speculation, it reported the police were looking at this possibility. An ex-colleague of Alison quoted her as saying her marriage had been 'damn rocky'. The husband, released after police questioning, looked on TV news a sad wreck, pining for Alison and describing their marriage as idyllically happy.

Television and the press carried pictures of Alison and her husband. And one day, to my horror, Alison's photo of me appeared in the tabloids.

Reporters began to crowd and harass me. I was accused of having a secret fling with Alison. Suspicion grew and the police hauled me in for a traumatic grilling then set me free with an ominous 'don't leave town…'

The quality of family life deteriorated fast – for all three of us – as months rolled on without resolution. Alison's husband made appeals for anyone who saw her to come forward.

For a time I vied with him for prime suspect status. I'd told the police about the man in the grey suit, but neither they nor the media showed any interest. Strange, maddening, worrying!

Eventually the hullabaloo abated and the reporters lost interest – as did the police. Thank God, from sightings reported to a Crimewatch programme had come belated evidence that Alison was alive after she'd left town. I got an official apology, media interest died locally and searches for the body were abandoned.

But all we main parties suffered. Her wretched TV producer husband couldn't find work last year and a few days ago stepped under a tube train. I'd felt rather like taking such action after Lyn and Janie left me. Couldn't blame them for leaving – the atmosphere in the house was nigh unbearable, with plenty of accusations and shouting. Three years ago Lyn found solace with a guy, and we divorced. I continued to see Janie once a month – but my daughter seemed lukewarm about our meetings.

Increasingly I'd sought comfort from the bottle. My employer lost confidence in me and I lost my job. Maybe this was the shock I'd needed. With some help from an alcohol counsellor, I picked up, got a better job and with half the proceeds from selling the old house, bought a flat.

I got by. But the empty silence in my flat became oppressive. I found myself pining, not for Lyn and Janie, but for Alison. In my dreams she was the one who turned me on. I settled into a bachelor existence that was humdrum and sad.

What could get me roused to stamping round my room was the notion that the elusive man in a grey suit could have got away with murder. The D.I. had listened when I requested an interview at the station. No, I had not imagined this. No, I got just one glimpse and couldn't describe him. Yes, I was sure Alison went off following him – despite the abject failure of CCTV to show this! The policeman's observation that a lot of men wore grey suits was not helpful. Politely containing my fury, I left feeling like I'd had a 'time-waster' snub.

* * *

Last week, something happened. The tabloid's 'ALISON LIVES' told the story. It reported she had walked into Thailand's British Consulate to give herself up.

Soon the essence of her story emerged in the press and on television. She'd made her disappearance as she'd become terrified of her abusive charming husband. With true identity concealed – change of name and passport – she'd lived in Thailand. After reading of hubby's death, she'd decided to end the mystery.

On return to the U.K. she was remanded in police custody overnight pending a court appearance. The media were mostly sympathetic. 'CONSPIRACY – TO DO WHAT?' asked one tabloid, naming this as the charge the police would bring. 'WASTING POLICE TIME – AND OURS', grumbled another paper. But the pro-Alison thinking prevailed. On her appearance at Bow Street Magistrates' Court – the public gallery packed with women vocal in her support – the police reported they were not bringing charges.

The women's groups weren't the only folk in the public gallery rooting for Alison. After her release, when the cheering faded, I yelled and attracted her attention.

A few minutes later we met outside the courtroom. Yes, she'd changed. Hair colour and styling, dress, even facial features (she'd surely had cosmetic surgery) were different enough for me to have hesitated. And, while she'd never been plump, she must have lost a stone or two. But I'd surely have recognised that cheeky smile.

She gaped at me. Then her eyes twinkled. "Bob – dammit!" She stepped forward to embrace me.

* * *

Now we're an item, living in a remote place. Alison writes freelance and I work part-time. Royalties will come from her semi-autobiographical novel, which her publisher trumpets as a future best-seller. I live every day with her to the full.

But there are unanswered questions. I still don't know exactly how she got to Thailand and survived there (as a waitress, she says) without the police tracing her. Having a brother 'high-ranker in MI6' surely helped her to vanish. (Yes, that man in a grey suit. I still haven't met him, and I've a feeling I never will). She gets quite paranoid and tearful if I touch on these questions. I don't *need* to know – and now my tale is told, I'll keep shtum.

Yet I can't shake off a bad feeling. Alison could disappear again!

ENDS

2. Big Hitter*

It was barely dawn on this mild but overcast January morning. The driver window open – to access a head-clearing rush of air – Joe sped through familiar countryside, his mind on the day ahead. Whirling right onto a country lane shortcut, he started from his reverie. A shout? Pumping his brake, he glimpsed in the rear mirror a dark-clad figure, looked like a man, lying on the road, rising to get onto one knee and stretching out an arm – towards a bike? Blast – had he winged the guy? He debated whether to go back and ensure the guy was okay.

Joe was good at figuring situations and taking rapid decisions. He decided. Guy seemed okay; nobody around to spot the incident; and he had to get to the meeting he was already late for. He accelerated.

Deep breaths, Joe. Shouldn't he have gone back, checked the cyclist was okay, given insurance details, rung work on the mobile to explain? Too late – decision taken!

* * *

Eventually he reached his space in Social Services' car park. Slamming the car door, he dashed upstairs for his meeting.

The Assistant Director's secretary greeted him. "Boss is incandescent."

Arriving twenty minutes late for an appraisal meeting with the boss was a bad idea. Joe's apology and brief excuse were dismissed with silence and a glare. After an hour that he didn't want to remember, Joe slammed the door as he left.

He'd worked damned hard to get to Principal Assistant – a 'catch-all' job where he got kicks from an abrasive Assistant Director and moans from Team Leaders he supervised. Still, his ageing boss would retire soon. And Joe, with his qualifications, experience, knowledge of the department and the ear of both Director and Committee Chair, was confident he'd land that job – however damning this appraisal report. Just twenty-seven, he was headed for the top. If not here, then elsewhere. The Director's "You'll be a real big hitter someday, Joe," had confirmed what he already knew.

The rest of the day was packed. Tackling a dispute between a Team Leader and her deputy, supervising the process of negotiated care packages, looking at resources needed for new initiatives, preparing stuff for Committee (well, for a burnt-out Assistant Director) were simple but time-devouring matters.

He finally escaped from the office into his car and switched on the radio. He froze, listening yet not wanting to hear. *'Police are anxious to contact the driver of a vehicle involved in a hit-and-run incident early this morning. An elderly man was knocked off his bicycle and taken to hospital, where he is in a stable condition'.* There followed mention of the location and an appeal for witnesses.

No! A hit and run! Elderly... hospital? The man hadn't looked old, or any way hurt. Joe turned left just before the exit and sat parked in an unmarked space, with engine and lights switched off. Deep breaths.

He knew what he should do. Walk into a police station and explain. What could he say in mitigation? He hadn't realised he'd hit the bike? No – they wouldn't believe that. He'd seen the man get up? No – the guy was in hospital. The bike hadn't shown lights? But it was dawn, and past lighting-up time.

He started at the tapping on his driver's window. He recognised the security guard. Joe wound down the window.

"Everything alright, sir?" Sounded apologetic.

"Yes. I'm thinking something through."

"Sorry to trouble you, sir. Safe journey, now." The guard walked off.

Joe wound up the window. Would look odd, him sat by the entrance. But why 'safe journey'? The man might have heard about the accident, but surely wouldn't suspect him. Unless the man knew where he lived? He glanced at his watch. 7.20. The Smyths were coming for a meal at 8 o'clock. And his journey took a half-hour.

He decided. He hadn't time anyway to go to the police.

Better check his 4x4 for anything incriminating, though.

He shone a torch over the front and side. Nothing visible. Thank God for the cow-bar – though maybe that was why he hadn't been aware of hitting the cyclist.

En route home, he stuck to main roads. With his temperature gage at minus two, he didn't fancy black ice on non-gritted lanes.

He got through his front door at precisely 8pm – to a smell of something fabulous, and to Katy. "Work," she said, evading his kiss and continuing to stir the soup.

Joe recalled his promise to be home by 6.30 – to read the babes their bedtime story. Katy would not rage openly, but she could freeze him out for days. "Sorry," he muttered.

The doorbell rang. The guests. Damn, must have been right on his heels.

* * *

At dinner, the wine helped him relax. Their friends were good company. The repast over, they adjourned to the lounge for coffee and a liqueur.

Joe sank into the armchair, lazily drumming fingers to the soothing background music.

Jean Smyth started the after-dinner chat with a comment that sent an icy blast through Joe. "That hit-and-run – did you hear?" She continued. "Maggie Green's grandpa, knocked off his bike, poorly in hospital. Maggie was gutted when she phoned this evening."

Max Smyth weighed in. "Police haven't caught the villain. When they do – hope they throw away the key."

Joe was glad the lights were dimmed. Somehow the rest of the evening passed. "Think I've drunk too much," he said, to explain his brooding silence.

* * *

The guests finally went. Joe turned to face Katy. "I'm guilty."

Katy frowned. "You are a villain, and hanging's too good for you."

Joe started. "Well –"

"However," Katy continued, her eyes shining in mirth, and drawing close to him, "You're forgiven, big boy."

"No – that accident, hit-and-run."

She pulled away from him and stared.

"You don't mean…"

"I do." He'd tell her everything.

"You *do* – oh my. You – Joe!" She sat down and slumped across the table.

He touched her on the shoulder. As she looked up, it hurt to see her cheeks moisten.

She drew her sleeve across her face and sat up straight. "What happened?"

He sat down opposite her and poured out his tale. As he did, he looked for signs of her reaction, but throughout she stared, stony-faced, unmoving. This was unnerving. For once, he hadn't a clue what she was thinking or feeling. "Well, that's it," he finished.

He swallowed as she continued to stare. Then she slapped the table with her hand and sat back, arms folded. Her angry expression boded ill and her words did not comfort. "Why didn't you stop? Poor old Mr Green. What if he dies?"

The sweat on his brow had chilled. Of course he should have stopped. How stupid and despicably selfish. So much for his idealism and humanitarian values! The old man was badly hurt – and, heck, might die. He, Joe, could have killed the man. And the grief he'd caused Maggie Green and her family…

Joe dropped into the armchair, bowing his head to search the carpet for inspiration. None came. Charges could range from 'failing to stop ...' to 'manslaughter'. Whichever, an inevitable prison sentence would end his meteoric career. Disgrace for him, ruin for his beloved family. Could he live with this – or indeed with not owning up?

Katy broke the long silence. "So early, it would be hard to see a cyclist not wearing luminous clothing and without lights." She rose, then flopped onto the arm of Joe's chair and leaned over, cradling his head.

He brushed his face with his sleeve. Katy's perfume and her now sympathetic approach were getting to him.

"Winter mornings – I hate them," she continued softly. "They're dark and miserable, and the roads are awful. I knew something bad –"

"Katy, the roads were fine this morning." The diversion was lessening the intensity of the situation. Joe decided.

"I have to go out," He rose from the comfort of the armchair and Katy's closeness.

"Why do you have to?" Katy's cheeks looked wet again. "You won't drive?"

He stretched down and silenced her queries with a kiss, then took her hands and raised her for one last hug. He grabbed his coat, got his bike from the garage and set off, pedalling swiftly along roads already gritted.

As a car swerved past him, he saw the irony of his situation. Great headline – 'Cyclist-hitter hit'. Divine retribution. And a way out.

He stopped by the river. Another option. He sat on the riverbank, shivering and watching moonlight dance on the water. He stretched out his weary frame, wondering at the stars.

Astronomers said there were billions. Could there be a life beyond this one? Katy believed there was. She talked about God, Jesus, love, repentance and forgiveness. And prayer. He'd listened and remained agnostic – though an automatic 'thank God' tended to slip out when he had any kind of narrow shave. Maybe a prayer wouldn't go amiss in this agony of guilt and indecision.

* * *

He took a few moments to come to. The water now reflected the deep darkness of a cloudy sky. Had he dozed off? He'd struggled at first in praying – expressing sorrow and seeking help from an Almighty he hadn't been sure he believed in. But now feeling calmer, he decided.

He drafted a final text message for Katy – a lengthy abject explanation, ending with an affirmation of undying love for her and the babes. Eventually he pressed 'send'.

Then, resolute, he cycled to the police station. He dismounted and strode in.

Big Hitter? Yes. But never in the sense he'd envisaged. A careless moment plus a bad decision equalled death to a lifetime's ambition and dreams.

ENDS

Published in Formby Writers' anthology 'The Day that Changed Everything' 2013

3. Crispin and Delilah

Outwardly earnest, Crispin chuckled inwardly. His sole companion in this first-class carriage was a most agreeable purple-saree-clad Indian woman called Anaya – somewhere in her thirties and a right stunner. She was making this otherwise deadly boring journey from Goa to Mumbai extremely enjoyable.

She really listened – her dark compassionate eyes widening in obvious appreciation. When he stopped talking, she gave a toss of her long black shiny hair, and smiled. "So, you are a very big man in business?"

He smiled back. "Well, I suppose I am." A hugely modest under-statement from a man who'd just stepped down as Chief Executive of an expanding multi-national, with a record pay-out that ensured his millionaire life-style in retirement. He added "I got to the top pretty fast and stayed there, in a highly competitive world." Yes, he was proud of his ruthlessness that stamped on rivals – but he wouldn't mention *that* here.

"Crispin, you must have earned this holiday." Did she flutter her eyelashes?

"I guess so – and after decades at the top, thought I'd let another guy have an innings." He laughed. A bit awkwardly. Though a fit 70-year-old, it would stretch credulity to ape losing thirty years. And he did wonder if he'd been outsmarted, nudged into resigning, via the Board's insistence that he'd merit this two months' all-expenses-paid Indian holiday.

"You have another career, eh? University professor?" She clapped her hands and gave a squeal of delight. "At my old university." Her gaze was unrelenting, consuming.

Well, the University of Mumbai were giving him an honorary doctorate and his lecture was being filmed and broadcast globally in several languages. "I suppose I have the highest academic recognition." He must get her to stay with him in the luxury suite for the weekend.

She clapped her hands again. "Gosh!" Those melting brown eyes, inviting.. "Your lecture – it is about business?"

"Yes. I will speak on 'Secrets of Entrepreneurial Success', and reveal vital messages to my audience." But he wasn't planning to tell them the maxim drummed into him from earliest days by his stern unbeloved father – the rule that guided him through shark-infested waters: 'Look after Number One and Trust Nobody'.

"Your lecture sounds interesting." She'd leaned forward, elbows on knees. Mesmerising perfume. He reined back an impulse to grab her.

"Would you like to go back to your old university, Anaya?"

"Ah, that would be…" Her face puckered.

Thoughtful-looking, she was even more desirable. "Then come with me as my guest of honour, Anaya. I'll get you the most luxurious accommodation, at the Taj Mahal Palace Hotel." She was staring at him keenly. Sure of this conquest, he leaned forward, stretched both arms across the carriage and grasped her hands.

"Hell…" His left hand and arm… on his knees … right arm flailing. He was in some kind of hold.

She was smiling down at him. She released his hand. "I hope I did not hurt? I do ju-jitsu."

"No problem," he managed – forcing a smile and regaining his seat (though scarcely his dignity). Damn the bitch! His bruised fingers would recover soon, his right knee maybe take longer. But he wasn't giving up on the chase. Maybe she'd show him a judo clinch!

The train was slowing. "I get off here. My answer is: No thank you, Crispin."

No! She'd reached the doorway. "But Anaya…" Ouch – that knee.

She pulled something from her bag and placed it on the seat by the door. "Crispin – this is my card. If you want to contact me, you must write." And she turned, to vanish along the corridor.

She knew all about him; he, nothing about her (except she'd given her name as Anaya). Anyway, a modern Delilah – who'd probably have demanded a fortune for sex.

Resting his leg on the seat, Crispin got out his pack of fags, lit up and focused on the smoke rings billowing towards the roof. Ah…at least he could smoke as much as he liked. 'No smoking' sign, but what the hell. He needed something after that roller-coaster.

He extracted his hip flask and took a gulp. That was better. A sharp nip in the thumb reminded him to stub the fag.

He spied her card, wriggled down the seat to retrieve it, and settled back to examine it. Well – be damned! He did a double take. Anaya Kakar was a shrink - and no ordinary one! A string of letters after her name and – '*Professor of Psychiatry, University of Mumbai*'.

He swallowed the rest of the whisky and settled back, stretching along the seat. Maybe her couch would be more comfortable than this. As he began to drowse, he chuckled, then heaved with laughter. Anaya Kakar was a damn good shrink. First woman ever to shrink his ego. He *would* write to her.

ENDS

4. Family Matters

"I've something to tell you, Jack." Ruth's face was one big frown.

"Go on." He swallowed. Was she leaving him?

"It's about Julie. She needs money..." Her voice trailed off.

Ah, their beloved daughter at a London uni. Might have known. "How much?"

"Two thousand pounds."

"TWO THOUSAND POUNDS!" Jack pounded the solid pine table. "Does she think we're made of money?"

Ruth flushed. "She was crying over the phone, Jack. She –"

"Okay – the waterworks," he cut in. "She sure knows how to tug the heartstrings. Not exactly the first time she's tried to bleed us – is it?"

"I know she's asked before – and yes, we have helped her…" She paused.

"HELPED her! That's an under-statement. She's had enough wet-nursing."

"Calm down, Jack. She's in a right state, beyond desperation."

"Look, we give her five hundred pounds a month. And she got that bursary. What on earth does she do with the money?" He pushed back his chair and started pacing – hands clenched by his sides.

Still sat at the table, Ruth drew a sleeve across her cheeks. "You know the problems she's had. She could be forced onto the streets to beg."

"At this rate, we'll be having to beg!"

"So you'd be okay with our daughter begging?" Ruth said quietly.

"Well – I didn't mean..." He stopped behind his chair, suddenly fearful.

"Jack, you haven't even asked about her plight." She blew her nose and wiped her eyes. "Our only child is in very deep shit." She looked up at her husband, now silent with brows furrowed. "Let's sit down and talk about this properly."

* * *

They'd reached the M1 in record time. No talk, just soft music on *classic fm*. Now, stuck outside junction 9, Jack kept silently swearing and cursing God. 'Incident', the sign read. 2p.m. and he'd have to reach junction 2 soon to get to Julie's pad in time.

He glanced at Ruth. Her head back, eyes closed – asleep or praying. At least he was now in the picture. Julie had got into debt, tried to recoup cash at the local casino, and was on a 'promise to visit you' from debt collectors. 'Two thousand quid by 4p.m. today – or we'll do you over'.

Jack hadn't stopped to figure what 'do you over' meant. A dash to the bank – and £2000 was in Ruth's ample handbag. He banged his forehead against the steering wheel, and slumped over it, inhaling from his sweat-soaked shirt. Maybe he should pray. "Please God, please," he whispered.

He was being shaken. "Jack!" Ruth shouting. He'd dropped off and the inside lanes were moving. He stamped on the accelerator, stayed in the fast lane, touched 90 as the traffic cleared, zoomed off the motorway and shot along the roads to Julie's.

Five-past-four. Damned lift wasn't working, so he and Ruth bounded up to the 8th floor and shot along by the railing to Julie's. Good thing they were both fit.

Julie's open doorway greeted them. Jack charged into the room to see their daughter being held, arms pinned by a large hefty-looking gangster type.

Jack heard a growled "What the hell," then Julie's "Dad, Mum." He focused on the giant holding Julie. No sign of a weapon. A glance at gangster number two – also big and mean-looking – confirmed he had a knife poised. Action!

Jack stepped up to number two, ducked the knife, and had the gangster face down, disarmed and bleating.

Julie had broken free, and Ruth had her captor in an arm-lock, pleading.

* * *

Holding out the cash to two shaken-up gangsters, Ruth said "We're Martial Arts Instructors. Scram forever! If you come again, you'll be carried away by ambulance."

The gangsters were scowling at her. Number two pocketed the cash then looked at Jack. "My knife," he demanded.

"NO!" Jack stepped up to confront him. "It's illegal to carry that. Just go."

Number two shrugged. "I don't need it, man." He turned to face the door. "C'mon," he growled to the bowed giant. The pair, affecting to saunter, walked out.

Not so cocky now, thought Jack, closing Julie's door.

Clutching Ruth and Julie in their hug, Jack felt the tears come – relief that his much-loved daughter had been saved from the gangsters. Thank the Lord that Ruth's love and persistence had forced him to actually listen! Today he, with Ruth, would continue to listen – and they'd damned well ensure Julie had enough support to steer clear of this kind of desperate situation.

ENDS

5. Funny Old World

I do not know him. I cannot see him. But I do know that he, Big Brother, is watching ME. I am walking home on this dark cold night – along cheerless ill-lit back streets. Apparently deserted, though shadows cast menace.

I round a corner and spy a figure propped against a wall and with legs sprawled on the pavement. A beggar – I see a large cap lying by his side. I zip up my anorak and pull the hood over my head. He barks "stop!" at me, springs up magically, and I know he is plain-clothes thought police. I try to run past, but my knees buckle and arms trap me.

"What the heck?" A distant voice, familiar. I'm shivery, scared, sweating, blinking myself awake. And Dot's arm is reaching over me, like she's grasping for something.

"Bad dream," I mutter, and turn to hold her close.

"You woke me, scared me – yelling something," she says, cuddling in.

"Sorry," I reply, feeling a spark of arousal.

She pulls herself free and sits hunched up, crossed arms clutching her shoulders. "You're boiling hot – and I'm freezing without the duvet."

"Sorry." I retrieve the crumpled duvet and reinstate it, then find I'm shivering – this time it's the cold.

My wife, now dressing-gowned, has switched on her reading light and holds up *Woman's Universe*. I have an inspiration. "My dear – I'm going downstairs for a pot of tea. You?"

"No. Why this sudden and uncharacteristically noble gesture?"

"I want to tell you about my dream – real scary."

She peers over her mag. "Scary! Save it. I've a nice story that'll get me shut-eye."

I shuffle down to the kitchen, sit on a stool, boil the kettle and put two tea bags into 'Wee China', our wedding present teapot. As the water streams gently in, I savour the aroma – surely mildly addictive – and wonder whether the before-my-time tea leaves smelled or tasted different.

Let me explain why I'm dwelling on this. I recently came across David Boyle's work titled '*A Funny Old World*'. This drew attention to English traditions that were *not* English in origin.

I decided to research into and write about one such: 'Tea-drinking'. Why that? Well, those of you who've read '*My Granny's Back Shop*', will recall that the rich welcoming aroma from innumerable cuppas, to countless friendly visitors, was a consistently happy feature of my childhood and adolescence, from the late 1930s to the early 1950s. Yes – sentimentality.

Among the many sources listed by David Boyle as references, was an article on '*A Nice Cup of Tea*' which was published in1946. This title grabbed my interest – so I googled it and read it through, with a feeling of incredulity. The author claims that tea is one of the mainstays of civilisation in the UK, and that the best way of making it can lead to violent dispute. He specifies eleven rules for tea-making.

Now here's what surprised me: The author with undoubted expertise on the subject of tea is none other than *the* George Orwell, creator of that most brilliant and haunting of satirical novels – *Nineteen Eighty-Four* – which depicts skilfully how society can decay under total authoritarian control.

Inspired to re-visit *Nineteen Eighty-Four,* I took it to bed last night. Before drifting off, I trod in the shoes of that stolid character, Winston Smith, as he was beaten and tortured in the process of being de-humanised. The stuff of nightmares!

To be sure – it is a funny old world.

ENDS

6. Ghost Writer

I didn't mean to scare her. But there she lay. I could tell she hadn't died, as I'd have sensed that. I suppose I hadn't known what to expect when I – her only daughter, re-visiting as a ghost for the first time – revealed myself. But for her to look terrified, scream, then faint, was a serious let-down. Honestly, Mother!

Back to being invisible, I floated by the ceiling as Mum came round, stood up, then sat with a cup of tea, propping her elbows on the kitchen table. I was debating whether to show myself again, when the front doorbell rang. Mum exited the room and I heard her say "go into the kitchen."

Enter Mrs Brown from next door. *Mum's best friend from before I was born, she gives me a warm feeling as she was good to me when I was a kid. And yes, I'd enjoy overhearing the gossip she would so expansively pass on to Mother.*

She plonked her solid frame down at the table for her tea and two sugars, got out her posh fags and lit up. *She always did this and I'd get these heady fumes in my bedroom long after she'd gone.*

"What's up, Meg?" she coughed out hoarsely, peering at my mother over rimless specs. *Yes – her voice sounds like an ailing foghorn.* "You look like you've seen a ghost." *Bingo! Full marks, Mrs B.*

"No, I just felt giddy earlier, but I'm fine now. Expect it's the cuppa and," Mum paused and smiled, "the company." *What! She's just glimpsed her beloved departed daughter, and that's all she can say! Still, Mum, maybe you don't want to risk getting seen as some crazy woman.*

Mrs B. lit up again and blew into Mother's face as the salacious titbit was delivered. "Julie over there," she nodded to a house across the road, "she's up the duff – and her only sixteen!" *Little Julie Smith – gosh!*

"Oh dear," said Mother.

Mrs B. moved closer to her. "And you know who the father is – they say?" she growled.

"No," said Mother.

Mrs. B. didn't keep Mum guessing. "Rory Grant."

NO! This must be wrong.

Mother looked concerned. "But Rory's such a nice lad. He was…" she paused as Mrs. B. leant towards her, "a grand little lad when he was younger." She reached for the teapot. "A top-up, Martha?"

I'd had enough, and streaked away towards outer space. Mum had been about to say 'He was Jenny's boyfriend'. But she'd stopped short. Since the inquest and funeral, in the months since I crossed over to the Heavenly Domain, neither she nor Dad has spoken my name. Not once! I know that, as when anyone on Earth mentions me, I get an immediate sensation alert. Tells me who that person is – though not what's been said.

* * *

First thing I did on leaving the galaxy was wire up to Baz, my Spirit Guardian. Every new fantie (as we phantoms call ourselves) has a Spirit Guardian to help them cope with the after-life existence. Baz has been great, taking me through the customs and rules of the Heavenly Domain.

While we're Spirits and invisible to humankind, we're allowed to reveal (i.e. show ourselves and talk) twice to someone we've loved – and once, for a haunting, to our most hated. The ultimate penalty for serious infringement is to stay Earthbound eternally in one place – and Baz told me of sad tormented ghosts stuck haunting, for aeons, literally.

I told him about Mother's fainting.

"So she was terrified at the sight of you. What guise did you adopt?"

"How do you mean?"

"Well, what do you think your mother saw?"

"Me, of course."

"Okay, but which version of you?"

Damn, I'd overlooked the first step of revelation – adjusting the image. Starting at point of death, we fanties can switch to reveal ourselves as we were – any time right back to new-born. "Mother would see me in my death agony."

"So you forgot." he said. "And she swooned! You're lucky. Point of death can be handy to bump folk off with shock – not just scare them."

"Thanks Baz. Next time I'll choose my image more carefully."

"And it's your last revelation to her," he reminded me.

* * *

I de-wired, and floated deep in thought. I must reveal a nice image to Mother. There was unfinished business. I decided to switch back to wearing my Graduation robes. Immediately after the ceremony had been indisputably a happy occasion, when both Mum and Dad radiated pride and contentment. I guess they too had achieved a first-class degree – in parenting. And I'd never felt closer to them.

When I floated into the house, Mother was washing the teacups. *Good – Mrs. Brown had gone. Only problem was the horrid scent from over-use of the clear-the-air spray.* Mum dried the crockery, put it on a tray and carried it through towards the china cabinet.

Suddenly she whirled round, shouted "No!" and hurled the lot against the wall – right where my picture used to hang. *Wow, Mum! Smashing stuff, but you gave me a fright.*

She collapsed into her easy-chair and started wailing – creepy noises, like hurt animals can make. Then she quietened and sat slumped, gaping towards the marks she'd made on the wall.

Time for action. I floated over to sit in the other easy-chair (Dad's) opposite her, and revealed myself. A few seconds of anti-climax passed before I realised her head was turned away – her gaze fixed on the wall. I rose to standing, then sat down again.

That had done it. She turned to face me, shut her eyes then opened them. She suddenly leapt up and flung herself at me. I went at speed to behind the chair. She sprawled over it, clutching the cushion and shouting "Jenny, Jenny."

I suppose I should have expected she wouldn't just settle down for a conversation with a ghost. I positioned myself beside the pile of broken crockery, then said gently, "Mum, I'm here in the spirit."

She was rising, and looked poised to lunge at me again. "Jenny," she called out.

"Yes, but DON'T try touching me. I'm not flesh. I'm spirit." *I thought Mother would understand.* "PLEASE sit on your chair and I'll move back into Dad's. There are things I want to tell you."

She looked about to spring, but retreated slowly into her chair. I floated across to sit in Dad's chair again.

"Look Mum, this will be the only time you'll see me. Please listen." She looked bemused. "I need you to know –"

"You betrayed me!" she interrupted. *I could feel her anger burning me.* "How could you do that?" she sobbed.

"Mum – I was very depressed, suddenly. I'm really sorry to hurt you and Dad so much. But I couldn't help it." *Yes, jumping off the top of a multi-storey car park hadn't been the smartest thing to do - but my mood had dipped to minus zero after Rory's horrible phone-rant dumping me.* Seeing she was listening, I added, "It was like being in a trance. Again, I'm sorry for the hurt. The second thing –"

"The coroner said it was suicide."

"Yes, Mum. I did kill myself. Something came over me and I suddenly felt life was hopeless – but as I was dying I wanted to live." *As I'd lain in agony and helplessness, I rued my fatal mistake. Surely the biggest of my twenty-two year trek on planet Earth.* "The second —"

"How could life be hopeless? You'd everything to live for!" *True, but I realised it too late.* Mum dabbed at her moist face with a hankie – her eyes still on me. "Why didn't you come to me? You could at least have rung, and we'd have talked."

I squirmed. "Sorry Mum. You were always there when I needed you. I guess, with going to Uni then moving south for the new job – well, I just didn't think."

"Your Dad and I went through hell." She bent forward, peering at me. "You say you're spirit, Jenny. Is this really you?"

"No and yes, Mum. I am a ghost, here once only, to tell you things I want you to know."

Her creased face looking calmer, she leaned back into the chair. "I'm listening."

The front doorbell rang, then I heard a growled whisper through the letterbox. "Can I come in?" *Not now please, Mrs. B.!* "I've something to tell you."

Without moving, Mother dealt with this overture nicely. "No, Martha," she called out. "I'm in the middle of something. It'll have to wait till tomorrow."

"It WAS Rory Grant," came Mrs. B.'s loud hoarse whisper. *Okay, I'll believe it. Psychopathic charmer!* There was a grunt and the sound of retreating footsteps.

Mother said "Go on, Jenny."

"Mum, it's great to hear you say my name. You and Dad just don't talk about me."

"That would hurt too much. Maybe we're still in shock. Your Dad's been working very hard, never says a lot anyway."

"Mum, I'd like you to start talking about me again – sometime soon."

She sighed. "Right, Jenny. I'll try to work on that."

I had an idea. "Look Mum, you know how Dad's always wanted to be a writer?"

Mum looked puzzled. "Well?"

"I think it might help him if he could know what's happened between us today. I could write this up – and add a few of my own thoughts."

She frowned. "I'm not sure how he'd take that. How could it help him write?"

"At least he'd know I'm okay, Mum. I'd write it as a short story. Might inspire him – and my Creative Writing module wouldn't be wasted."

"Alright – but I'd want to check it over."

"Mum, I'll arrange for it to be on that laptop you share with Dad – in the study. Tonight, when you're asleep. Cut out anything you're unhappy with."

* * *

After the goodbyes – when I conveyed messages, about loving her and Dad and my being okay in the Spirit world – I floated away. Baz said that to write the story on the laptop, I'd have to risk revealing again and breaking the rules. This would automatically go to the Heavenly Court for a hearing.

I don't care. I *will* clear the unfinished business with both my parents.

Also I've decided to use the haunting visit. In my death agony guise, I'll reveal to Rory Grant. I doubt it'll kill him – but he might behave better towards women in future!

ENDS

7. Hearing Voices: A Reflection*

I sometimes 'hear' the voices of folk who've made an impression on me. Like my dad saying 'Billy, use your common sense', or my wife's 'I love you, Bill'. Such internalised messages can replay in my head. I don't actually hear the voices.

Have you ever actually heard a voice you can't account for anywhere in the environment? I never have. But I've known many folk who have done. Most of these I met several decades ago while working in the mental health field. They were really hearing voices that were troubling – unwanted intrusions they hadn't invited and couldn't control.

Some years ago – as an aspiring fiction writer – I wrote this short piece:

VOICES

Lazing in the sun's warmth, lying elbow-propped,
Infused with the scent of new-mown hay,
Hearing the stream babble.
"You're no good, Frank..." **My teacher's voice** *within.*
"Drown yourself." **That Voice** *from without. Insistent.*
Sitting upright, I check quickly around – field and stream.
Nobody.
"Drown yourself!" **That disembodied Voice** *again, now*
commanding.
I'm no good, and **that Voice** *tells me what to do.*
But I'm zonked. I lie back on the soft grass, struggling to
order jumbled thoughts.
Drowsy, I'm being shaken. A familiar perfume, engulfing.
And **Isabel's voice.** *"Frank – wake up. Thought you'd*
died. Love you."
The Voice! *I raise my head to meet her strawberry-*
flavoured lips.

In this piece, **that disembodied voice** was one which might lead the hearer to seek professional mental health support. And Frank's inner, internalised voice showing such low self-regard could make this the more likely.

More recently I've become friends with others who clearly do not need or wish psychiatric help. Each of these is deeply religious and spiritually aware – and feels blessed to have heard the voice of God. I am a Christian, but do not appear to have been blessed in this way.

And surely there are other reasons why we can hear unexplained voices. In each instance the experience will be different, though the form and the nature of the content may be similar to myriads of others across the globe.

Sometimes the hearing may indicate a special gift, which carries extraordinary sensitivity. This can be experienced positively or as a kind of burden.

Sometimes unexplained voices may be down to physiological/neurological factors affecting the ear and/or the brain. Our design and functioning as human beings are so amazingly varied and complex that it's hardly surprising these factors often continue to baffle specialists.

Interested readers – especially any troubled by hearing unwanted voices and needing support – might care to visit the Hearing Voices Network: www.hearing-voices.org 01142718210. This offers useful comment on a range of experiences that can be puzzling, sometimes scary – and gives information about a network of Hearing Voices groups.

ENDS

Published in 'Formby Bubble' 2017

8. Illegal Immigrant

The management seminar has been a bore – scarcely worth the day in London. But the feast in this restaurant has compensated. The bill paid, I start towards the exit.

My stomach tightens. He sits at the table ahead, reading a menu. As I halt, staring, he looks up towards me, and I see that distinctive birthmark adorning his /left cheek. Boulding's grey-blue eyes meet mine. I feign a cough and, turning my back, retreat with head lowered – between tables and into the toilet. I lock myself in the nearest closet, fumble for my handkerchief and mop my brow.

We met eight years ago. Everything from then is so vivid. I re-lived it many times and I do so again now.

I'd sat in a small room – sweat damping my brow despite the draught from the air conditioning. Mr Boulding, grey-suited, sat interrogating me from behind a desk. He was large, with furrowed brows and grey-blue eyes whose gaze I could not hold – and blond hair he kept smoothing back. My eyes kept being drawn to a birthmark on his cheek, which I saw as a sign of his humanity.

"You face deportation." He held up a hand to silence my protest. "We must detain you overnight, and I will see you again tomorrow morning." He nodded to the policeman in the doorway.

Escorted by the policeman, I stumbled out and gulped at the air as we returned to the van. I'd been in the room for most of the afternoon. There had been breaks in interrogation while Boulding left the room. Perhaps he went for refreshment or a smoke, or to check something I'd said. But I was required to remain, shifting on an upright wooden chair as my back and my bum ached.

I jolt from my reverie at a creaking noise.

It sounds like the outer toilet door swinging. I hear footsteps. Could this be Boulding? I check the closet door is locked. Thank goodness this closet is solidly enclosed. There is silence, then whistling. I hear footsteps fading, the outer door swinging. Silence. Phew! I check my watch. I could not have been here more than five minutes. Better wait a bit longer.

I am again back eight years ago.

After seeing Boulding I was locked in a cell. Through the night I railed with fury at each of the four walls. Had I any hope of leniency from this man who barked out stern questions and listened sphinx-like to my pleas?

I re-played what I had told Boulding. My father, a politician who became a minister of state in Sri Lanka, got me English tutoring when I was aged six. He said it was a passport to a prosperous future. From my local primary school, I went to Colombo's best school. I gained university entrance and came to the UK to study civil engineering.

I then suffered many misfortunes. Soon after I'd enrolled, my parents died when their house was bombed. Devastated, I flew back for the funeral, met my few surviving relatives, but did not linger in Sri Lanka. I returned to the UK to continue my studies, and completed my first year successfully. Early in the second year of my course, I had glandular fever for a few weeks and couldn't attend classes. I scraped a pass. Towards the end of my third year the fever recurred.

Also my year-long relationship with Usha had broken down and I'd had to move to new lodgings. I was really depressed, even felt suicidal, and missed the final exams.

I applied to the Home Office for an extension to stay in the UK and was granted this for one year – to complete my course. I was having severe financial problems, absented myself from University and found two casual jobs – as a restaurant washer-up in the evenings and as a builder's labourer in daytime. Payment for each was weekly – cash in envelopes. I felt forever tired, had no social life and lost all will to study.

The year went by, then another. I changed lodgings three times, found different casual work (just as miserably paid). But I tired of living 'hand-to-mouth' as a fugitive from the law. This was barely existing – in a state of poverty and fear, not truly living. I went into a police station and disclosed my illegal status. I was taken to another building – where Boulding had interviewed me.

So – I'd told Boulding my story. And the next day I was back facing him.

We sat in that same room. I was again sweating despite a current of cool air. Boulding repeated an accurate outline of my story and asked if I wished to add anything.

I'd decided to be contrite and plead for leniency. I told him how sorry I was to have offended against the law, that I admired everything British, and desperately wanted to stay in the U.K. I stressed what happened to my parents, and said I could face death if deported. (Yes, I did fear for my life if I went back to Sri Lanka. Another relative had recently been targeted).

I sat back. I had done what I could. I watched him carefully, awaiting his judgement.

He gazed at me – his elbows on the desk, his hands together, as though about to pray. I felt those grey-blue eyes piercing to my soul, and I trembled inwardly. Then I fancied I saw a smile. Was this a prelude to sarcasm?

"Well," he said, "you can apply for asylum." He proceeded to outline grounds upon which such application might be made.

He stared through me. "I doubt that your case would be strong, given your failure to use the year's extension, the passage of time since your parents were killed and the current Sri Lankan government's improved record on human rights. But you've a right to try." He stooped to fiddle with his briefcase, then handed me a sheaf of papers. "This is what you need. Read the instructions. If you complete the forms now, I will forward them for consideration." He rose from his chair. "I'll be back in an hour." He left me – the policeman remaining as sentry.

On returning, he took back the forms, and put them into his briefcase. "As you voluntarily disclosed your illegality, I'm inclined to use discretion over whether to have you detained." He secured my promise to report each Monday at the named police station, and dismissed me with a wave of his hand.

But I never did report at the police station. That night I did a runner. Packing my belongings, I left London, caught a bus to Leeds – and never, until today, did I return.

My re-playing ends as I hear the toilet's outer door creak.

Heavy footsteps approach and the neighbouring closet door is shut and bolted. I listen carefully. Is it Boulding? Don't think so – grunts are too high-pitched. But I decide to leave anyway, as staying too long might attract attention.

My plan is to make for the restaurant exit rapidly with head bowed, feigning preoccupation. If he follows me, I can run fast.

I approach the toilet outer door. As I reach for the handle, the door swings towards me at lightning speed, knocking my hand. In a moment of terror I see the imposing bulk of Boulding inches short of colliding with me. I halt, rooted. It is the showdown – and I face imprisonment or exile.

"I'm sorry old chap," Boulding says in a 'nice guy' voice. "Are you okay?"

Shaken, I nod – still awaiting judgement and arrest. I feel shame, as a cheat who has betrayed trust placed in him.

He stands there in the doorway, blocking the exit, inspecting me. "Are you sure? You look knackered."

"I'm okay," I confirm, head bowed.

He holds the door open, gestures me through. "I'm glad."

I am back among the tables, again heading for the restaurant's exit. My relief begins to surface. He hasn't shown any sign of recognition. Then I doubt. Could he have been pretending? Or might it suddenly come to him?

I walk quickly out of the restaurant to my car – half expecting to hear running feet and a cry of 'stop'! Approaching my car, I look around. Nobody is pursuing me.

As I drive home to Leeds I keep glancing in the rear mirror, let cars overtake. I do not see anyone following me.

On the long journey I continue down memory lane.

When our relationship collapsed, Usha and I had agreed to stay friends. She'd caught this religious thing when she went with her female best pal to Student Christian Movement, where a visiting preacher got at her. I'm Muslim, am happy with my faith – and I guess I'd exploded when she kept on trying too earnestly to convert me across!

After she'd graduated and gone back home to Leeds, we'd remained friends and kept up contact periodically by mobile phone.

Every time she'd ask if I was 'alright'. Though I'd always said 'yes', I was far from 'alright', failing academically, stressed, overworked, feeling unwell, and dodging the law as an 'illegal' in London.

After Boulding released me that day, I had rung Usha. She said I'd surely end up being deported (which echoed my foreboding), and wanted to rescue me. Brilliant girl – she'd rung back with a plan. Her daddy, a builder, would employ me as a labourer. Within the Asian community she had a friend who would give me shelter. So I went to live in Leeds.

* * *

Now, some years on, I have a new identity. Soon after I'd got to Leeds a wheeler-dealer friend of Usha's father arranged this. He was apparently repaying a favour to her family.

I am manager across two of Usha's daddy's building sites. In my spacious apartment, I live alone. But this is about to change.

Usha, having married her fiancé two years after I'd gone to Leeds, has divorced him on the grounds of adultery – a charge he did not contest. We are now engaged to be married. She, with her adorable four-year-old daughter Christina, will soon be coming to live with me.

She says she never stopped loving me, and was sorry when we broke up. We agree that our love is strong – and that we will respect our different faiths. While I don't intend to change, I might sometimes accompany her and Christina to the 'happy' church they seem to enjoy. Family unity I see as important.

I so like Britain. I must stay here. I bless Boulding. But I do not think I will ever re-visit London!

ENDS

9. Joan's Funeral

"Joan's died."

The phone message was cruel and unreal – and a dreadful start to the new millennium. Cousin Joan was three months younger than I, but her ginger curls blue eyes and slim figure made the age gap seem like ten years. Only last year she had rung for a lengthy heart-to-heart. She'd sparkled with news of early retirement and an impending Caribbean cruise.

"Cancer – only diagnosed three months ago." Cousin Ronald spoke in whispers, croaking and sounding hesitant. I struggled to match this with the tall athletic ex-basketball player and fluent story-teller. I guessed he was in a state of grief – probable in the light of his lifelong closeness to Joan.

We three, each an only child, were cousins because our respective mothers (all long deceased) were sisters. After her parents drowned in a boating accident, eleven-year-old Joan moved to live with two-year-old Ronald and his parents. Ronald had told me of his shock on discovering, just after he'd made a speech at his eighteenth, that Joan was not his sister!

Listening to Ronald's account of Joan's illness and death, I felt sad that I would not see her again. As children we'd played together and been good pals. A survivor of childhood illness and teen bereavement, she'd grown into a pleasant and mild-mannered woman, with a gentle sense of humour and a keen social conscience. Contact between us had for decades been largely by postcards and Christmas cards.

Then about eight years ago her apparently rock-solid (and childless) marriage had ended suddenly with husband Dan's revelation that he was going to live with another woman and their baby.

Melancholy and, I suspected, some dependence on alcohol, were then evident in her occasional lengthy late-night telephone calls. Over the past two or three years she'd sounded happier, and the rambling late-night calls had ceased.

As Ronald's stumbling narrative continued, I had a second shock. For over three years, he explained, Joan had lived with a partner, Ben.

"What!" I interrupted. "Who's Ben?" Then, as Ronald continued, I realised I'd actually met the guy. On our last visit, not long after Dan left, my wife Kathy and I spoke to Joan's next-door neighbour Ben, over the garden fence. A short fiery-looking middle-aged man with a mop of fair hair and a trim goatee ginger beard, he had given generously of his views on politics and education. Kathy and I had agreed – neither of us liked this boring aggressive man.

"She died intestate." This third shock didn't seem so bad – more something of a mild surprise. Ronald was now his articulate self. "Ben's a swine. Didn't want you to know about the death. Demands the house – says that would have been Joan's wish."

Ronald explained he and his wife Sheila had seen a lawyer. Ben had no legal rights, and should vacate the house, leaving the contents untouched. Ronald and I, plus any other surviving cousins, would, as nearest relatives, be sole beneficiaries of Joan's estate.

Ringing Ben that day to start discussion about the funeral, Ronald had also relayed the lawyer's advice. He said Ben shouted and swore, calling Ronald and me evil money-grabbers, vowing never to leave the house and saying he could produce a hundred lawyers in his support. After two hours of what he termed 'the mother and father of rows', Ronald had put the phone down.

"You sound a bit traumatised," I said.

"I'm okay, though I took a battering. That guy's a phony and a thug – and there's no way he gave a damn for Joan." He paused, as if to draw breath. "And that's not all. The funeral's a problem."

I sighed, still reeling from the impact of the bad news so far. What next?

"Joan used to be Methodist, should be buried with her folks after a church service. Ben simply proposes going to the local crem, and cutting out a church service. I suggested sharing funeral costs, but he insists on paying the lot. The snag is that he's the one on the spot, with all the contacts."

He went on to describe how he and Sheila had seen Ben bullying Joan. "He's a psycho. Kept shouting abuse at her. She was scared of him."

Feeling hurt myself, I managed to end the call.

* * *

An hour later, while Kathy was helping me debrief, Ben rang. In oily cultured tones, he introduced himself as Joan's partner. He gave an emotional account of Joan's being ill and dying – stressing her wish I should not be told of her illness.

I listened, grunting only occasionally. Then I mentioned Ronald had phoned.

"They're beneath contempt, he and Sheila. Wicked fools went straight to a lawyer. I'll give Ronald a good hiding," he shouted. He swore undying love for Joan, asserted his absolute moral right to the house and his intent to repel with force any attempted entry by us or anyone else.

Numbed and resentful at the impact and content of the two phone calls, and dismayed at the hardening adversarial stances, I enquired about funeral arrangements.

At this any remaining veneer of civility disappeared and the volcano erupted. "That f…..g Ronald, and now you!"

My protestation went unheeded.

"You b…..s think you know best. I'm the only one that knows what Joan would want." After a further tirade directed against Ronald, he calmed. "The funeral," he ended authoritatively, "will be at our local crematorium, and I will arrange for a non-religious ceremony. No mumbo-jumbo."

I heard his receiver slam down. I sought more TLC from Kathy. I still couldn't really believe Joan had died. I reflected on our last long conversation, and rued not arranging to meet up.

I agonised, as Kathy listened. Why would a legal secretary not make a will? Could that have been deliberate, if Ben was bullying her? I fought against the dislike and distrust beginning to envelop me. Perhaps Ben had helped Joan feel happier. The timing of Ronald's relaying the legal advice was insensitive, and a grieving Ben's explosive resistance understandable.

* * *

Ben rang with the funeral details. At the crematorium, his humanist friend Edward would oversee a celebration of Joan's life, and a buffet meal in a restaurant would follow. He surprised me by asking if I would speak briefly about Joan in childhood.

Flattered, I agreed – but added that Ronald might also want to say something.

This provoked a vitriolic response, with derogatory comment about Ronald.

Days of apprehension followed. Hatred between Ben and Ronald seemed mutual and irrevocably deep. I didn't much like either of them.

Ronald's telephone outbursts now focused partly on the funeral and Ben's determination to keep total control over the arrangements. "It's heathen – not a proper service." His lawyer had advised against attempting anything legally, and he tried (unsuccessfully) to enlist my support in jointly confronting Ben on the issue. His overriding concern though, he kept emphasising, remained that Ben should 'not get one penny'. Apart from the legal position, he'd seen Ben humiliating Joan.

Ben's phone calls were abrasive and rambling, with no pretence at civility. I should not be getting anything from the estate as Joan hadn't liked me. Ronald was a 'miserable piece of shit' whose claim to a share couldn't be justified despite Joan's declared affection for him when they'd been young.

Fearful, I kept imagining dreadful scenarios, with rows over funeral and intestacy threatening to desecrate Joan's memory. Nightmares punctuated the little sleep I was having.

* * *

It was sunny for the 200-mile journey down motorways to the 1.30pm funeral in London. An hour early at the crematorium, we espied Ronald and Sheila (who had travelled by train and stayed overnight locally). They looked and sounded upset.

Other mourners joined us – friends of Joan, relatives of Joan's ex-husband, a few other folk I didn't recognise.

Finally a short stocky man with straggly fair hair and greying ginger beard arrived.

"That's the b....r," muttered Ronald, nudging me.

I stepped forward to re-introduce myself and Kathy to Ben. He stiffened, grunted, then glowered at Ronald. I thought for a moment fisticuffs would ensue. But thankfully Ben turned and strode away to greet someone else.

* * *

The 'celebration' was a positive appreciation of Joan. Her former boss and I paid verbal tributes, and others read lyrical passages. In my oration I reflected in humorous vein on the first encounter Joan and I had (at Joan's home, shortly before her parents' tragic death) with stone-throwing two-year-old Ronald. I noticed Ben laughing and Ronald dabbing at his eyes.

After, in the crematorium grounds, Kathy and I spoke with Sheila and Ronald.

"Never thought I'd say this," said Sheila. "That was nice, entirely about Joan."

A strained-looking Ronald said he had to agree – though he'd always regret it had not been a Christian service. "But Joan'll surely be in heaven."

We all agreed. Our God was loving and just!

At the buffet, to a background medley of Joan's favourite tunes, there was a buzz of friendly chatter. Acquaintances were made or renewed and contact details exchanged, anecdotes were told, and food and wine were consumed.

I was surprised at one point to see Sheila and Ronald talking with Ben. Apprehensive, I kept glancing over while one of Joan's friends, Helen, told me about their trips to the theatre. The dreaded encounter ended with handshakes.

* * *

All that happened four years ago. The journey thence – through mourning and conflicting interests to the final legal settlement, was not hassle-free, but much less difficult than I had feared. Ben vacated the house – moving his stuff back to next door. Ronald and I jointly administered the estate, discussing with Ben and varying the settlement to accommodate him equally and bequeath to Joan's favourite charities.

That the anticipated bloody battles were avoided and compromises so easily reached could be traced to the funeral. Before it, war seemed inevitable – with the very shape of the event a contributor. Then the experience of reflecting communally about Joan seemed to have a transforming effect, leading to the softening of stances.

* * *

Although the process of recalling and writing has given them immediacy in my mind, the events belong to a different era.

As soon as his money came through, Ronald bought a villa on the Costa del Sol. He and Sheila retired to this new abode – and I haven't heard from them since.

After the funeral buffet I'd warmed to Ben. I came to believe he really had been fond of Joan, and was truly grief-stricken. Maybe the story of abuse could be interpreted as his effort to control Joan's drinking – and her declared happiness (talking about a holiday she'd been on, though without mention of a companion) in our conversation six months before her death, had sounded refreshingly genuine. So I'd invited him to spend a short break with us. A year later he'd taken up our offer.

Apparently our hospitality extended to his seeking and appreciating Kathy's TLC. Two years ago she moved out to live with him in London.

And me? After Kathy's departure, more acrimonious exchanges with Ben and subsequently sorting out material things with Kathy, I took my bruised self to a Retreat for a week. I came home re-charged but lonely and badly needing TLC. You'll recall that at the funeral I met Helen? We're now growing younger together.

ENDS.

10. Life Sentence

Rob lounged in his armchair. The year 1991, he was back in the UK after forty years - and the secret was still his.

Mentally he replayed that departure from Scotland.

Aged nine, with Mum and big sister Rosie (his elder by five years). After a near-sleepless night of bad dreams, Rob remembered crying as he'd turned for a last look at home on that frosty November morning.

"It'll be good, Rob." Mum's words of reassurance as she gave him a cuddle in the airport-bound taxi had seemed at odds with the tears on her cheeks.

On their flight to Australia he'd got comfort from Mum's cuddles and soothing words. Fatigue too had helped dull the sensation of intrusive images from the recent nightmare.

Being reunited with a bronzed-looking Dad at Melbourne Airport had been good. He'd gathered Dad was Professor of Architecture, something to be proud of.

But Rob had feared that meant Dad would change, a worry that grew over the months the latter had been away in Australia. The feel of Dad's huge enveloping arms and the warmth of his greeting had begun to reassure him. The car was bigger than before, but that was good as he'd snuggled into a luxurious back seat.

A shrill whistle interrupted his reverie. The kettle. He'd forgotten he was making tea.

Absentminded professor, he thought. This was wholly accurate now – Professor Robert McIver Nisbet, who'd always been a bit absent-minded. He wandered to the kitchen, and returned to his armchair with a steaming mug. He checked his watch. Alone for another hour or so. He'd meant to work on a paper. But that gloomy feeling left him unsettled. Sipping the hot sweet liquid, he returned to his memories.

"Our new home!" He could still hear Rosie's high-pitched yell as the car slowed. At last he too could feel excitement. Guilt and fear were ebbing. And in succeeding weeks the welter of experiences adapting to new surroundings and people helped with these dark feelings that had been overwhelming.

The early weeks at the new school had been rough. Playground chants of 'limey, limey' on that first morning were a precursor to being shoved to the ground and spat upon. Vilification and being punched were bad enough, but the ostracism had been the worst. Boxing lessons from Dad helped him sort out the number one bully – after which his 'street cred.' soared, and acceptance as 'one of us' began.

He smiled as he recalled the practice in his bedroom at moulding his Scottish brogue into some form of Australian accent. Later a talent for cricket earned him plenty of respect among peers.

After a shaky start, and a need for extra support from his teacher and Mum, his schoolwork soon proved well above average. At University in Melbourne, he'd warmed to the academic life, getting a first in Chemistry followed by a PhD, then, as research associate, post-doctoral work.

He'd loved working in a field that had, from childhood with a chemistry set, fascinated him. A lecturing post at Melbourne followed, then a senior lectureship supervising post-grad. programmes.

Chimes – melodic. The clock they'd acquired with the house here in Bromley.

For each step up he'd faced tough external competition. And with enhanced status had come greater awareness of academia politics and back-stabbing. Increased pressure on the University to cut back on pure research for that favoured by the drug companies had been resisted initially and later accepted as something to take on board. He was, though, selective – determined to use his talents only for projects that he saw would benefit the human race.

His application for the Chair at the neighbouring rival institution had failed, against a younger guy with a lousy research record. "More entrepreneurial than you," the panel chairperson had muttered to him as they parted. *Damn – spilt tea! He gulped the remainder. Should have been his job!*

That was a few years ago. Would have been good for all the family too. It had been 'dead man's shoes' at his uni, with the Prof a contemporary. Rob had settled again to teaching and research.

Throughout, he'd occasionally re-lived **that night**. Sometimes it was a nightmare and disturbed sleep, but worst were the haunting flashbacks. There were periods of gloom and wanting to be left alone brooding, re-playing the scene and the 'what-ifs'. Now he was in the UK, the flashbacks were more frequent.

He glanced at his watch. Half an hour before Lil would return.

Ah, Lil. Super-wife. From their first meeting at that party, when he'd accidentally jostled this attractive young woman, she'd been a true soul-mate. Nice humour too. "I *am* lily-white," at introduction – then, with a smile, "but to you I'm Lil."

Months later they'd married and set up home. They'd postponed having children while Rob pursued further academic qualification and Lil earned as a teacher. Then, after years of futile trying and near despair, Daniel was born. What joy!

His eye wandered to the large framed family photo – Lil and Dan in the centre, and himself with one arm around her, the other around Rosie, and his parents on the other side next to Lil. Everyone looked happy.

He sighed and his eyes moistened.

Within a year after the photo, tragedy – his parents killed in a car crash and sister Rosie dying from an aggressive cancer. They'd been a close family – though he'd never told any of them **his secret**. He hadn't even told Lil. He'd nearly done so a few times, but fear of consequences kept him silent.

He winced on recalling the uncomfortable poignant moment at Rosie's deathbed when, staring at him, she'd gripped his hand and murmured, "That night." Startled, Rob had queried, "Rosie, what about that night?" but she'd relaxed his hand and died.

He'd wept, grieving at the loss of his beloved sister, and had for a time tortured himself wondering what she had known about **that night**.

Now, nearing fifty, with Lil having left teaching, and Dan nine, Rob was back in the U.K.

Headhunted to apply for Professor of Chemistry and departmental chief at this prestigious university in London, he'd done so reluctantly, then waltzed successfully through the interview. He'd wanted to stay in Australia – even without any kind of promotion – and had no wish to return to the island of his crime.

Lil was compellingly keen – made it clear she'd love to settle in the UK. And Dan's changing school wasn't problematic. He'd been bullied and slumped in performance this past year – and voiced loud enthusiasm at the idea of moving to Britain. So here they were, in their new home, with Dan enrolled at school for September.

"Hi – it's me." *Lil was back, and he'd spent the whole time reminiscing!*

* * *

A few more days passed, then Lil said "I want to go to Strathtoon – to where you grew up."

"I'm not fussed about that." Rob feigned diffidence. "There isn't much to see and there'll be nobody I know."

"Surely you'll want to re-visit the place you grew up - show us your old home, where you played and went to school. You've told me a lot about it all."

Yes, thought Rob, but not about **that night**.

"Besides," she continued, "Dan's the same age you were when you left. It would be great for him to go there before he starts school. He and I are both dead keen."

Yes I'd have liked to take them, thought Rob – also struck by him and Dan being a similar age when uprooted for a trans-global marathon – but I don't want this.

"You're scowling, Rob. What's wrong?" asked Lil.

He dragged up the obvious excuse. "Well, I've still a mountain of preparation to do – and people to meet."

Lil's face had reddened. "I thought you'd be pleased to show us your childhood haunts. I am bloody disappointed in you!" Throwing her cushion against the wall, she ran out.

Heck, she never swore, and he was the one with the temper!

Rob wrestled with his inner demons. He was a coward. He considered rationally. Which was worse – visiting Strathtoon or hurting Lil and Dan? He sought out Lil in the bedroom. "Let's go north tomorrow. Just stay overnight. Okay?"

As they embraced, Rob wondered whether to reveal his secret. He and Lil had no secrets from each other – except (as far as he knew) this. But shame and fear kept him silent.

* * *

The long car journey north to Strathtoon was exhausting for Rob. His head throbbed despite the paracetamols. Even driving, which he usually enjoyed, didn't help. He envied Dan his sleep of innocence. Lil looked strained and pensive.

* * *

The following morning, from their hotel, they walked around the centre of Strathtoon. The town's main street, with its solid stone buildings, looked pretty well unchanged to Rob, except that everything seemed much smaller – and the polluting traffic was noxious.

"We're gonna get the best ice cream in the world," Rob told Dan, and both were disappointed to find Janetta's now Duffy's D.I.Y.. A search for comics took them to the newsagent, where the face of the red-headed gaunt man behind the counter looked familiar. Of course – Alec something, in the family business. They'd been pals.

"Alec?" asked Rob.

"Aye – who're you?"

Rob reminded his former playmate.

"Och – Specky," said the man with a smile. "We used tae play fitba' in the playground. You've grown a wee bit." He handed over the ice creams. "But you jist vanished. It was a funny thing." He hesitated, looking hard at Rob. "Ah thought at first ye were deid."

Rob laughed, though he was feeling vaguely uncomfortable. "I went to Australia – and it's a good job I did, or I wouldn't have met Lil." He nodded across the shop to where Lil was looking at the comics with Dan.

"So you escaped to Australia, eh?"

Smiling back, Rob squirmed inwardly. 'Escaped' was so true. The guy was probably making conversation – but could he know something? "We have to move on," he said, and buying the chosen comic, ushered Lil and Dan out of the shop.

Next he took them to his old school, and recounted stories. Lil kept smiling. Dan asked a question or two then started yawning.

"Where did yah live Dad?" drawled Dan.

Lil joined in. "Come on Rob, we want to see it."

Rob led them through a maze of streets to a cul-de-sac in a leafy suburb. "I played a lot of football here," he said. "Doesn't look big enough now." These houses that had loomed towards the sky looked almost too small to live in.

"There." He pointed to a house in the corner. Dan leapt to the front gate and Lil walked over to join him. Rob followed, remembering ruefully his last look forty years earlier. Lawns had given way to bricked patio, but apart from the door colour and the size, the house looked the same.

"Can we go round the back, Dad?"

"No, I think we should leave now," said Lil. "That upstairs curtain's twitching."

As he followed Lil and Dan out of the street, Rob felt his stomach tighten. He must have a look. "Lil, you take Dan to that wee shop." He pointed to the sign. "I want to check something round there up the hill. It's boring. See you at the shop in a minute."

Leaving them – Lil open-mouthed – Rob sped round the corner and up a hill. He halted, shaking with fear then disbelief. The burning warehouse was no longer there, of course. But in its place was a leisure centre. He stood staring at the space age style creation, trying to gather his thoughts.

"What's this about?" Puffing and red-faced, Lil had followed and Dan was at her heels.

"Well, it's a long story."

Dan agitated to go in, but settled for a promise of 'tomorrow' – and a visit to 'that wee shop'.

* * *

That evening Rob told Lil.

Two days before he'd flown to Australia had been November 5th, and that evening he'd been taken by sister Rosie to the nearest open space – a concreted playground next a large warehouse – to let off fireworks.

Besides the bought fireworks, Rob had secreted under his coat his homemade 'special'. Rosie had met a boyfriend, and it was while they were snogging in the nearby shelter that Rob had wandered and propelled his rocket towards the warehouse. He'd looked on with pride, turning to horror as he saw a flame arise then dance high in concert with others. He'd run to the shelter where Rosie and boyfriend were cuddling.

"What's up?" Rosie had asked, pushing her boyfriend away.

"Dunno. Somebody's lit a fire." Rob pulled at her sleeve and pointed to the flames across the field.

"Let's go, Rosie. Might cop us for it," he'd heard the boyfriend say. As they rushed downhill and round the corner, he'd seen a fire engine then heard a police car siren.

It was Rob's bedtime when, shaking, he'd reached home. His nightmares as he tossed and turned were of sirens and police cars and fire engines – and he'd tried to block them out by burying his head under the bedclothes.

The following day he'd heard Tam ('ma dad's a fireman') Reid holding court in the school playground. "There wis flames up a hundred feet – folk screamin', burned alive." Rob had shrunk away. The rest of the day had been a blur, then home, bed and off to Australia early next morning.

"I was shocked and traumatised. Nobody else knew." Rob paused, remembering his sister's dying words. "I don't think even Rosie – she never said. I couldn't tell anyone. Going to Australia helped me bury it – 'til it seemed like a bad dream from long ago. I've been scared of the disgrace. Sorry I didn't tell you. Can't bear Dan knowing I'm a criminal – and a fraud." He felt his eyes moisten.

Lil came over and embraced him. She too was crying and he felt the comforting warmth of her body as she clung to him.

Then she disengaged and sank into the armchair looking up at him. "You know – all these times you went into a mood and kept denying anything was wrong, like you had a secret!" She smiled. "For years I worried about an affair. Poor Rob. What a burden. Why aim it at the warehouse?"

"It was impulse. Maybe something to do with feeling overlooked and missing Dad. I'd no idea it would set the place on fire."

"It all sounds very innocent, Rob. How were you to know that one simple firework would start such a dreadful fire?" She stood up. "Let's cuddle on the settee."

As they sat together, Rob felt a wave of relief. Thank God he'd shared with Lil. He'd worried needlessly about how she would react. He was no longer alone with his secret. And how selfish he'd been! In his 'moods' he hadn't thought of the effects on Lil. "Sorry for my moods, darling. I'd no idea, never had an affair."

She snuggled up closer. "Thanks Rob." She kissed his cheek. "What next?"

He knew what he must do, and told her.

* * *

She held his clammy hand as next morning he went into the Strathtoon police station to see a senior policeman about the warehouse fire.

"Dad wants to see someone," Lil told a questioning Dan. "We'll go to the leisure centre after."

Now, as Rob left them to accompany the policeman, he carried the image of them sitting by the station's front desk – Dan studying his comic, Lil sitting erect, her face creased with worry.

"Take a seat, Professor. How can I help?" The Inspector leaned back in his chair.

"I have a confession," said Rob. He paused and looked up. The Inspector was now leaning forward looking at him – a penetrating stare – and frowning.

"Yes, sir?"

Rob swallowed, held the man's gaze, and spoke. "Forty years ago – the warehouse fire on bonfire night. I started it. Fired a rocket. I didn't mean any harm –"

The Inspector held up a hand. "Stop, sir!" He coughed. "You are confessing to a very serious crime. I need to caution you, and take a formal statement. I'll get a colleague to join us." He stood up and left the room.

Rob sat back in the chair and wiped his brow. The 'serious crime' would be arson – with goodness what penalty, even though it was historic and accidental and he'd been young. His fall from grace would bring shame on Lil and Dan.

"Inspector says he'll be back in a minute, sir," said the constable who had now come in to lean against the wall near the door.

Rob nodded and managed a grunt. The minute was an age. He thought of Lil and Dan in the reception area. What would they be going through?

The door swung open. "You can leave us, Jones," said the Inspector, and sat down opposite Rob.

What was this? "You said –"

"I know, Professor," the Inspector interrupted. "Now listen." He propped his elbows on the table separating them. "I've looked at our records. You did not cause the fire. The warehouse was burned down, but nobody got hurt." He proceeded to tell an astonished Rob that the night watchman had confessed to setting the near-empty warehouse alight. It had been accepted as accidental. A carelessly tossed cigarette end ignited some inflammable material.

"But I saw the flames start when my rocket landed." Rob scratched his head.

"Ah, yes. The report mentioned a wee fire there in the evening, on bonfire night itself – a few hours earlier. The blaze that burned down the warehouse wasn't until around one a.m. on the sixth November." He paused, then leaned forward. "That wee fire had looked dramatic, but because the rocket landed in the rubbish bin, it came to nothing. The fire service and ourselves had been called, and soon dealt with it."

The Inspector smiled. "We'll not be prosecuting for that."

Rob let out a "Whoopee," grabbed the policeman's hand and pummelled it. He turned and floated out of the room back to his waiting family, and shook with laughter and relief as he hugged Lil.

His life sentence had ended.

ENDS

11. Life-Changer

Danny tasted sick. He blinked his eyes half-open, then shut them. That light! And a hammering inside his head. Peering through heavy eyelids, he made out vague shapes. The smell was pungent, unfamiliar.

A tidal wave of pain struck as he tried to raise himself. Something or someone was restraining him, and he heard a voice. "Don't move." Who was this – and where was he?

"You're on a drip." Now he made out the blue uniform of a nurse, staring down at him. What on earth was he doing in hospital? In pyjamas?

"What –" he began. Then retching tore at his guts!

The nurse removed the bowl of sick. "You must have banged your head on the floor." She paused. Smiling? "When you fell off a table."

Her peppermint aroma was nice, and familiar. "What – where?" His head was packed with splintered wood. And he wasn't seeing properly – nurse looked hazy. Maybe this was a nightmare?

"When your friend rang –"

This was weird. "Who?" he interrupted.

"Your friend – from the pub."

It came back, flooding. The pub – his celebratory night out with best pals Terry and Steve, starting so dully with a couple of pints, hotting up with a few liqueurs. And he'd stood on a table, making a speech.

"How're you feeling?" The peppermint again. Like Joanne. Joanne?

"Joanne!" he yelled, pain giving way to panic. "Look, I've a plane to catch – 11.30 this morning. Must get there."

"It's midday," said the white-coated man who'd appeared beside the nurse. "And you're not fit to go anywhere. I'm sedating you."

As Danny felt the jab in his arm, he cursed helplessly. His secret tryst to elope with Joanne was no more.

ENDS

12. Lonely and Grieving

Sue took another gulp at the gin bottle, lit up a fag, and dialled.

"Samaritans – can I help you?" A man's voice, Irish maybe.

Sue waited. She didn't know where or how to begin. She fumbled with the paracetamol packet.

"You're still through to Samaritans. Take your time." The voice sounded friendly.

But Sue felt unable to respond.

"My name's Pat. Tell me – are things bad for you now?"

"'m Sue – yes." You bet things were bad. Despair had been followed by loneliness – and now again there was despair. As she'd downed a fair amount of gin, coherent speech was proving difficult.

The voice continued. "Anything you say is confidential to Samaritans."

She wished she had rung earlier. She started crying, then sobbing. She flashed back to exactly one year ago. Dosed with painkiller and semi-conscious, she'd seen the fireman as she was cut from the wreckage – and came to, helplessly drugged, in a hospital bed.

"I'm still here. You're sounding real upset?"

Sure. No prizes for that, Mister. First anniversary of the crash that killed her beloved hubby Mac – 'upset' didn't quite describe her feelings. Still, this man was trying to be helpful. She tried to speak. "Mm I am…" No good. She was thinking clearly but her voice sounded weird as she struggled to pronounce words. The tears had dried.

"Could you be feeling like ending it all?"

This man was good, maybe psychic. Sue tried to tell him so, but could only groan.

"You sound in pain?" The voice radiated concern.

This TLC by remote was just what she needed. Tears were flowing again. Sue tried. "Wanna die. Mac."

"Have you taken anything – like tablets?"

"No, 'm drinking." Thank God she could speak again.

"Is that why your voice is slurred?"

"Yes."

"And tablets?"

"No." She'd tell him. "But – gonna take paras."

"Sue, I'm hoping you won't reach for these. But it's your life. Look, I'd like to hear how life's got so desperate for you. I've plenty of time. Could you maybe tell me?"

She started "Year 'go, Mac…" she wanted to tell him, but the tears were choking her. "Can't speak…"

"I'm not going anywhere. So you and Mac were very close?"

"Insep'rable…" The sobs were coming. "Sorry…"

"No need to apologise, Sue. Sounds a terrible time for you. Look, it might be easier for you to talk in the morning. Would you like us to call you then?"

"P'r'aps."

"If you were to give me your phone number, I'd arrange for this. A Samaritans colleague would ring to ask how you're doing, listen and talk with you. They'd shred your number after – so you'd stay anonymous. How about that?"

Sounded like they cared. Nobody else did. She slurred out her number, and agreed they could try between eleven and one o'clock. She'd probably be dead by then. She managed to replace the receiver.

She gulped at the gin, drained the bottle, and almost set her sleeve alight trying to strike up for another fag. She reached unsuccessfully for the pack of paracetamols, knocked over the gin bottle and blanked out on the carpet.

* * *

Sue's unconscious state was far from blissful, with a series of nightmares. In the last of these, she was driving and turned to Mac, who smiled at her. There was a bang, and Mac was flying off into the sky.

She came to, sweating. These nightmares! Sometimes she was in the car, sometimes lost in a desert, sometimes in a strange dark place – all with Mac leaving her alone, scared and helpless.

She inhaled the reek of gin. And her nostrils twitched with another familiar smell, quite comforting. But the urine had dampened her thighs – not so pleasing. Where was she? Lying on my back, she deduced. She tried to move, and felt her head explode in pain.

Dosing semi-conscious, she had pictures of happier times. She could see Mac sorting out that bully who'd name-called her. She could hear her friend Gemma yelling "A right James Cagney." Then a heart-stopping thrill as Mac turned round and asked if she'd go out with him. Her – Sue, always a wallflower – at seventeen!

Must get up. Her exploring fingers felt her living-room carpet and a bottle that was unbroken. She struggled to look up then shut her eyes tight as they encountered an inverted blue triangle of light. Ah, the curtains parted at the top. Stiff and sore throughout her being, she managed to raise her head gradually, then hoisted herself onto the chair. She groped for the paracetamols and washed a couple down with a mug of cold tea she'd made earlier.

* * *

Showered and changed, Gemma sat in the conservatory with poached egg on toast, a fresh mug of tea and a ciggy. Mac smiled at her from the photo on the table – and she was able to smile back. Somehow, 22nd June – this dreaded first anniversary – had passed.

"We're on the second year now, Mac," she said to her smiling late husband. How she missed him! Teenage sweethearts, her rock – the one man in her life and the only one she'd learned to trust. She couldn't at first believe he had died – and the eventual verdict 'heart attack, probably at impact', hadn't much helped with her anger that he'd deserted her.

She replayed in her mind the happenings of the previous day. It had started with her visiting Mac's grave and laying flowers. Then she'd lain on the grave, talking quietly to him about the plans they'd made. "We'd be on the plane to Jamaica now," she'd murmured. Sometime later, she'd stood up. "You should be here," she'd yelled as she turned away.

Then straight home. She'd started looking at the few photos of her and Mac, and the memories were so vivid and moving.

If only Mac had been driving. She'd insisted they pull into the service station to change drivers. If only that lorry driver hadn't swerved from the inside lane into her path.

And so it had gone on. If only Joey had lived. They'd waited till their mid-thirties to try for children. Then the joy of finding she was pregnant was blanked out. Vain efforts to induce her necessitated a caesarean – and Mac had been forced to choose between her and the baby. They'd named him Joey. A perfectly formed little man – she'd demanded to hold him and hadn't wanted to give him back to the nurse.

Sue lit up another cigarette and drew heavily on it. Her cheeks were damp! Such was their sorrow that they gave up trying for children. Mac was busy on the international banking scene. She'd taken to reading women's magazines and went back to work at the bank.

This morning, she was feeling more at peace – certainly not suicidal. The talk with that Samaritan had helped. Maybe there was a way through the mourning. The man had sounded genuinely concerned, and she'd warmed to him.

The phone was ringing. "Is that Sue?" A female, soft voice, young-ish.

"Yes. Who's speaking?" Could Samaritans be ringing *her*?

"Julie from Samaritans. You spoke with Pat last night. How are you now?"

"Better thanks – last night I wanted to die. Say sorry to Pat. I was drunk."

"That's okay. Pat thought you were trying to ease pain. I'm glad you're feeling better. He also thought you'd be more able to talk now about what's wrong."

She wanted to. Encouraged by Julie's enabling prompts and queries, Sue told her story. Halting and tearful to start, then confidently.

"What's the worst thing for you now?" asked Julie.

Good question. "The 'if onlys' plague me. Maybe that's inevitable when I'm grieving."

"I wonder if you've thought of short-term counselling – maybe via your G.P. – to help with that?"

She hadn't. "H'm, could do, thanks. But even worse is this aching empty void. I miss Mac so terribly, and I've no real friends. All our friends were other couples. Only time I go out is to shop, and I get home as fast as I can. Then I'm lonely, brooding."

"That sounds so understandable, Sue. I hope that someday you'll feel able to pursue interests and maybe experience some joy. Remember that when your mood dips, you're welcome to ring and a Samaritans volunteer will listen and try to support you emotionally– we're 24/7 and it's free to call. How did you hear about us?"

"Shopping. The store's notice-board. Something about distress – and your number 116123 leapt out at me. A life-saver. Thanks Julie, to you and Pat."

* * *

The second anniversary of the crash. Nothing like as painful as the first. Cognitive behavioural counselling had helped with the 'if onlys'. She'd go into work, and in the evening lay flowers on Mac's grave. The other anniversaries – marriage, his birthday – were likewise a mix of sadness and celebrating the happy memories.

While she still missed Mac terribly, she could also feel his presence – somehow spiritually, she reckoned – encouraging, playful. And when at all lonely she'd speak to him – there 'in her mind's eye'.

She'd also spoken to Samaritans a few times –
though not for several weeks. The conversations had
helped to get her life back on track – and via the interests,
she was now making her own friends.

She'd found the card that nice woman had left her
after she'd got back from hospital. 'Holy Trinity Church
Pastoral Visitor – Ann Smith'. Sue had appreciated the
visit, but made it clear she'd never been a churchgoer.
'You're very welcome anyway', the woman had said.

So one Sunday months ago, she'd gone, sat
through the service, been encouraged to go for coffee in
the church hall after, and was indeed welcomed. She'd
got involved in their Christian fellowship, sensed rather
than knew God was there, and attended a bible study
group – determined to deepen her faith. Jesus Christ was
her martyred hero, with messages of love that could make
for a different, much better world.

She'd increasingly felt moved to help people in
distress, and, knowing she had a kind of gift for listening
to others' woes, she'd applied to join Samaritans and
been interviewed. Now, opening her post, she read the
letter and whooped with joy. She'd been selected for
training.

Her eye caught Mac's smiling face in the photo. "We're going to work with Samaritans, my darling."

Her life had really begun with Mac. Now it was taking off again!

ENDS

13. Mini-Sagas*

(a) BYE-BYE FUN

Happy being stretched, to the limit and beyond. Super exercises and games.

Great camaraderie, fellowship. One for all.

The T.A. was fun.

Off to the front. One for all

Suddenly: mangled bodies, pals exploding.

Shock Horror Terror. Bye-bye, fun.

He'd tell you himself but a bullet's just taken him out.

(b) THE COSTS OF BATTLE

He'd been determined to fight to the end. A battle he'd surely win.

Yet he was cornered, guns poking into his back.

"Raise your hands in the air," he heard.

Slowly, quivering, he raised his hands.

"Prisoner, put your hands in your pockets! You owe us winnings," yelled his grandchildren.

Tales in 50 words (excluding titles). Fun to make up!

14. Mission

I snuggle onto a seat on the platform of the deserted railway station. Shivering, I adjust my skirt and raise the collar of my coat. Jeans would have been warmer.

I see the uniformed man approaching me. He breaks the silence, with a steady measured step. I switch my gaze, to study the concrete by my shoes. My fingers tighten around the handle of my kitbag. Deep in my jacket pocket, my toy – Di, as I've named her – nestles coolly in my left hand.

The man looms over me. "What are you doing here at this time, ma'am?"

Stay calm. I gaze up at him. *He's big. I'll try to humour him.* I force my face into a smile. "Can't you see I'm out training for a marathon run?"

The man removes his cap and scratches the back of his head. "Funny way of training, ma'am."

This man does not do humour. I change, to looking at him earnestly.

The man replaces his cap. His face looks stern. "Anyway, you cannot stay here, ma'am."

But I know I must stay here, in order to fulfil my mission, when the London train hurtles through here in 10 minutes' time. *Ignore the 'Ma'am'. Persuade him.*

"Sir, I'm happy here. I'm not harming anyone. Please – it's so peaceful."

I hear a wheeze as he puffs out his chest. "I cannot let you, or your bag, stay on our property. You must come with me, ma'am." He makes to grab my arm.

Confrontation time. I whip Di from my pocket, point her at his chest. "Back off, Mister. Hands in the air." He complies, slowly backs away up the platform.

I hear the train approach, stand up, adjust my explosives belt, and step to the edge of the platform. I close my eyes, poised. *I'll jump and press the button. Now!*

But a human whirlwind crashes into my side, propelling me back onto the platform, the express thunders by, and my head thuds against the concrete surface.

* * *

I'm lying flat, being jostled. *Journey to paradise?* Through the haze a female voice says "You're in an ambulance, madam – en route to A & E – and we are your armed police escort."

ENDS

15. My Therapist Said

My therapist said it could help to write about this. Though years have flown since the happening, every sordid detail is embedded in my memory. Starting to write now, I feel that shivery tingling sensation in my scalp. *This* is my tale:

Dong – dong – dong – dong – dong. The Holy Trinity church clock across the way from my bed-sit startled me. It was a wonderfully melodious chime, which could also be damned intrusive when you're trying to get some sleep. Yet something wasn't right. I'd heard eleven, midnight, one, two (when I'd stopped swotting for my 9am exam, to down a coffee laced with glucose), and three, but not four. I looked at the textbook open on the desk I was hunching over. Still on page 121. I'd nodded off. Not too amazing as the dogma was mind-numbingly boring – and with last-minute cramming, I'd not had a massive amount of sleep lately.

Stuff this! Bed beckoned. I'd just hope the right questions came up. I yawned and stretched my arms. What was the weather doing? I leaned over and peeked through the curtain-less window. A clear sunny June day, and I'd face another scorcher in an exam room starved of ventilation.

A bit of fresh air now would be an idea. I stood up, opened the window and inhaled deeply. Ah – honeysuckle. Why couldn't they have the exams at this time of day, when it was cool, and my head was clear? The grand old church building looked at its best, awesome yet welcoming as the stone glinted in the rising sun. And the door was open.

The door was open? At 5am? And someone was lying on the steps! I did a double take. Yes, a body. Sprawled face down in a funny unnatural kind of posture. Lifeless. From the long red hair, probably a woman.

Better go over and investigate. But, peering more closely at the doorway, I fancied I saw a figure move. And with something in hand – looked like a gun. No, I wasn't going there. I reached for my mobile and dialled the emergency number.

A shrill voice asked, "Which service do you require?"

"Police – there's been a murder, I think."

"Please wait while I connect you."

I kept my weary eyes trained on the crime scene. Grim-looking. Could be more than one guy in the background. What was this delay? I sat on my bed.

"Police." A gruff male voice.

I told the policeman what I was seeing.

"Your name address and telephone number please, sir."

"I'm Dan Jones. My –"

"Your *full* name, sir."

"That *is* my full name. Why are you wasting time with this?" I didn't mean to yell, but in my sleep-craving state I didn't care too much.

"Because, sir, we've had a few too many hoax calls recently. And I must warn you – the penalties under the law for this, and for supplying false information to the police, are severe! So, your address, phone number, and occupation, sir."

Big mistake to shout at the police. "Sorry." I speedily gave my personal details, including my status as a second-year student.

"Are you ringing from your address, sir?"

"Yes." Get a move on, Plod, I thought, or the body'll be a skeleton. "And officer, can the police come quickly, as I'm sure the murderers are still inside the church."

"Sir, we will not delay in getting to the scene. Please stay where you are."

No problem there. Duty done; and I'd had enough of life for the day. I set my alarm, rolled over and stuck a pillow over my head.

* * *

Cannons were firing. I struggled to a state of semi-consciousness. Ten-past-six - and someone was giving the front door a bad time! A hammering that demanded a response. I heard the landlady's shrill "Who is this?" a muffled conversation, then the front door being opened. More conversation, whispered.

Footsteps started pounding up the stairs, as the landlady yelled "Police – for you."

Damn – that murder! Of course, they had to interview me. I swung from bed, sprang to the door and flung it open.

Two guys in uniform confronted me. "Can we come in, sir?" Undoubtedly a command.

"Surely, but do you have to see me now? I've an exam –"

"Yes," one policeman cut in. He puffed his cheeks, and I sensed trouble. "Our armed response unit have swooped, to find the church locked and – after gaining access to the interior – without trace of a body anywhere. We're placing you under arrest, on suspicion of making a hoax call to our emergency services and wasting police time."

A few minutes later, after my temper and self-restraint – not to mention my ability to stay awake – had been seriously tested, I sat, handcuffed, in the back of a police van. At the police station I protested my innocence. I was an honourable citizen who put himself out doing his public duty. The police should widen their search for the body.

I kept pleading with them – even swearing occasionally. But they wouldn't believe me. "A nutter," I heard the desk sergeant bark. Then they stuck me in a cell. I'm sure they detained me for hours so that I'd miss my exam. Squatting against a wall, I kept dosing off.

Come mid-day, they released me with a caution. Maybe Dad being a magistrate helped.

* * *

Thirst for the truth about that body has got me into attending the church. Regularly – in fact I'm now in a team that greets folk and equips them with service sheets and hymn books. But I know there's something fishy, as whenever I mention the body, people look strangely at each other, clam up and drift away. And one day a guy drew me aside, whispered that an ex-warden in his dotage would sometimes go into the church at night – and that the church used to hold a mid-summer pageant. While all that is interesting, I reckon they're trying to throw me off the trail.

But they won't. I tell you – what I saw *was* a dead body!

ENDS

16. Rocky Road

Act 1, Scene 1 – At the Breakfast Table

Jean and Ken sit at table after Grandma has left to take their two infants to Nursery.

KEN: (*Lounging, elbows on table, sighs*) "What's the matter?"

JEAN: (*Sitting upright across table, staring hard at Ken*) "You tell me. What *is* the matter?"

KEN: "What are you getting at?"

JEAN: "You know."

KEN: "This is crazy."

JEAN: "Goes beyond crazy."

KEN: "What does?"

JEAN: "If you can't figure…"

KEN: "What?"

JEAN: "It's over."

KEN: (*Sitting erect, frowning*) "What's over?"

JEAN: "Us!"

KEN: (*Rising, grips the table*): "Good heavens. You mean…"

JEAN: "What time did you come home?"

KEN: (*Stands, scratches his head*): "Dunno. The afternoon do at the office went on, and as the boss…"

JEAN: "You had to stay, and keep on drinking. I'll tell you what time. 4.37 a.m. you stumbled from a taxi."

KEN: "Never!"

JEAN: "Where were you?"

KEN: "At a mate's – Harry's. Needed to sober up."

JEAN: "Liar. I rang Harry's at 2 a.m., and he spilt all. So it's *her* again." (*Stands, points to front door*) "Go!"

KEN: (*Clasping hands in supplication*) "Come on, Jean. You can't mean that."

JEAN: (*Stamps her foot*) "I DO! I've had more than enough of your philandering. Just GO!"

    Sound of front door being opened, slamming. Ken and
               Jean freeze.

GRANDMA: (*Shouts from hall*) "Coo-ee, love-birds!" (*Flings door open, bursts into dining-room*) "Chicks safely delivered."

KEN: (*Turns to face his mother-in-law*) "Ma…"

GRANDMA: *(Stands looking at Ken, then Jean)* "Mind you – not without a wobble. Emmie didn't want to go in. Said she's got a headache. Little madam tried to kick me, then tugged my skirt. Hung on." *(Laughs)* "I was thinking – good job I've got my knickers on. Anyway…sorry I came in on your canoodling."

KEN: "Ma –"

JEAN: *(Interrupts, forces a smile as she goes to hug her mother)* "That's one reason I wear jeans, Mum." *(Lifts kettle, glances at Ken)* "Tea all round?"

* * *

Act 1, Scene 2 – Grandma Muscles In

Grandma seated at table with Jean and Ken.

GRANDMA: "This is a nice cuppa, Jean m'dear. I needed warming up. Now, my chick-a-doodles, what's the matter?" *(Nods to Jean)*. "Ladies first."

JEAN: "Mum, Ken's been unfaithful. He was with his lady-friend last night and –"

KEN: *(Interrupts, bangs fist on table)* "I'd been at the works do, Ma..."

GRANDMA: *(Eyes Ken sternly)*. "You do **not** bang my table! Wait your turn."

KEN: "Sorry Ma."

JEAN: "Yes, he'd been at a works party. It got late – 2 a.m. I was worried and rang his friend Harry (lives on his own, so at worst it woke only him). I got from him the tale of Ken's betrayal. He's a philanderer, Mum. He must leave!"

GRANDMA: "Remember – I decide who leaves, m'dear. If anyone. But what's this philandering, young man?"

KEN: "It's nothing, Ma."

JEAN: "What! Shagging another woman – and that's nothing?"

KEN: *(flushes)* "This isn't fair, Jean."

GRANDMA: "Now chick-a-doodles, let's stay calm. How's it not fair, Ken?"

KEN: "The works do went on. Got drunk, I'm afraid. Shared a taxi with Ginny Smith, our office secretary. She asked me in for a coffee –"

JEAN: *(Interrupts)* "And you started shagging her."

KEN: "No! She made me coffee. Strong, so's I could sober up – and we talked." (*Pauses, takes a deep breath*) "Look, I have a confession. I'd had a fling with this woman – one time when I'd drunk too much. But we'd agreed to finish it – and all we did last night was talk. I'm really sorry and won't ever see her outside work again."

JEAN: "Huh. I'll bet."

KEN: "Honest, Jean. It's you I love. I promise – no more philandering, ever."

GRANDMA: "I'm sad, chick-a-doodles. I'd never have guessed about all this. You've always been so lovey-dovey. Jean, you've heard Ken say sorry. Can you forgive him?"

JEAN: "I'll have to think about that. I'm still shocked."

GRANDMA: "Well, meanwhile nobody has to leave. Sort it. Remember your chicks."

JEAN: "Okay Mum. At least I know something I suspected." (*Looks sternly at Ken*) "In the true Christian spirit I forgive you, big boy. I'm hurting though, and I'll have the antennae out for a while."

KEN: "Thanks Jean. Might skip works dos in future. You and the kids are what matters."

GRANDMA: "One big happy family." (*Stands*) " Must have a nap before I get the chicks."

* * *

Act 1 Scene 3 (*One year later*) – *A Sad Event*

Jean sits at table with her two children - 3-year-old Emmie and 4-year-old Tom.

EMMIE: "What's happening, Mummy. Are you crying?"

JEAN: "You're only three, darling, and you might find this difficult…"

EMMIE: (*Stamps her feet*) "Mummy – I have to know!"

JEAN: "Well, darling. Grandma's just gone up to heaven."

TOM: "Mummy, do you mean Grandma's died and we won't see her again?"

JEAN: "Now, young Tom…" (*Pauses, dabs at her eyes*)

EMMIE: "That's not true." (*Tries to hit Tom and misses*). "You're wicked!"

TOM: (*pulls a face*) "No I'm not. Tell her, Mummy."

JEAN: "No, Tom's not wicked. And he's right. Grandma's died – and left us to go to heaven."

Both children start crying and run to their mum. Jean hugs them closely, and sobs with them. After a time Jean dries everyone's tears. They talk about Grandma, who was always kind.

TOM: "Where's Dad?"

JEAN: "He's working abroad – far away, in America."

Both children look glum.

EMMIE: "I want my daddy."

TOM: "So do I."

JEAN: "He's a very important man, your dad. He won't be able to come back for quite a long time. He'll miss Grandma's funeral." (*Hesitates*) "But Uncle Harry's coming."

EMMIE: "I like Uncle Harry. He always brings us sweets."

TOM: "So do I. He comes to play football with me."

JEAN: "He's a good kind man. A real friend."

TOM: "Yes. He's my favourite uncle."

JEAN: "Now children, Grandma's funeral is soon. Do you want to come – or to go to Great-Aunt Edith?"

TOM: "Will the funeral be sad, Mummy?"

JEAN: "Yes, but it's also to hear good things about Grandma – so many people loved her."

EMMIE: "Will there be cakes and lemonade?"

JEAN: "I'm sure there will, after we've come out of church. Will you go?"

TOM & EMMIE: (in chorus) "We'll go!"

ENDS

17. Teen Love

Heart pounding, seventeen-year-old Grace approached Reception.

"Can I help?" asked the trim-looking woman.

Averting the penetrating gaze, Grace put the 'one-month-free gym membership' voucher on the desk.

"Take a seat," said the woman.

Grace slumped into an armchair. She saw her reflection in the wall mirror opposite. 'Fat slob' – Mother's cruel cut in yesterday's row – rang in her ears. Okay, her plumpness contrasted with Mother's beanpole figure, but the comment was derisory and surely not accurate.

She looked at the floor – lost in negative reflection. What was she doing at a gym? She'd never been athletic. She'd always been overweight – and P.E. at school had been a nightmare subject she struggled to endure.

"Hello – Grace?" A deep voice, resonant. She gasped. A golden-haired youth was crouching beside her, smiling welcomingly.

He stood up, retreated a step. "Guess I startled you. I'm Mark, an instructor."

"I *am* Grace," she smiled, blushing and feeling a thrill as she gripped Mark's hand to help her exit the low armchair. She followed him into a small office.

This was dream-like – sat opposite a stunningly attractive man giving her undivided attention. Face burning, she talked – about managing her asthma, deciding not to re-take A-levels (she *was* youngest in her class), getting a job in the bank, winning this gym voucher in a raffle.

Mark's gaze was steady. "You won't remember me, Grace. You were in the year above at school. I left at sixteen, came here." He grinned. "Skipped A-levels."

She searched her memory. A blond-haired blue-eyed boy, cherubic and under-sized. He'd grown up fast! "I do now – I think…"

"Folk don't recognise me now." He laughed. "I've sprouted – and I'm twice as broad. It's the weight training."

She felt embarrassed stepping onto the scales, but Mark noted down her weight without comment – then took her blood pressure.

"Normal," he said. "Now your pulse."

Heaven loomed. Avoiding eye contact while Mark pressed her wrist, she pictured them holding hands.

"Seventy. Fine."

She trailed Mark on a 'walk to see what's on offer'. A store of inviting wonders unfolded for her. Well – a swimming pool that might scarcely have passed for the public baths. But a sauna, a Jacuzzi – and a tanning room! The gym held intriguing machines; and women straining at these varied amazingly in shape, size and age, with one hugely bulkier than she. Mark said little, and kept smiling warmly at her.

Back in the office, Grace arranged to see Mark next day for her programme. She floated home. *Her* instructor. The stuff of dreams.

* * *

Next day the programme was tough. With Mark's encouraging presence, Grace started warming up on the treadmill.

After ten minutes the sweat poured – and she was glad she'd worn a vest underneath. But that pong – my goodness, it was from her. She saw Mark's nostrils twitch. Quick thinking needed. "I'll just be a minute," she said – and rushed to the changing-room. After cooling and cleaning with cold water soap and towel, she glanced in the mirror. Her face stared back red and bloated.

Back to the gym. But where was Mark? Momentary panic ceded to jealousy as she saw him over in the corner, whispering animatedly to a young woman, a Diana of the slimming posters. He waved at Grace, and in a moment was with her.

"Okay? It's hard when you come to it cold." He smiled. "And Grace, when we break sweat, each of us has our own special scent. I happen to like yours."

Wow! Was he trying to be nice? No, seemed genuine. "Thanks."

"Let's go." He led her through a range of upper and lower body exercises – light on weights, few repetitions. Mark demonstrated, supporting her with nice words.

A big moment came with the abdominals. Lying on her back, she hesitated as she saw her tummy protrude. She blushed as he knelt by her and held both her wrists to re-align them for gripping the abdo cradle. Those eyes again. But surely he couldn't really care for her.

"Any questions?" she heard after the routine ended.

"Think I'll improve?"

"You're a bit overweight."

She'd swear her heart stopped beating. "Only 'a bit'?"

He straightened his shoulders, and his eyes shone with a mischievous glint. "Grace, if you can come at least three times a week, we'll soon have you losing the few ounces to peak fitness."

She smiled, and so did he. "That'll give you a challenge then, my *young* schoolmate," she quipped.

He grinned, rubbing his hands. "I'm gonna love this challenge."

In the changing-room and aching, Grace showered and dressed. Within her were stirrings. Something volcanic she'd never experienced before – an overwhelming attraction to this man. First guy ever to show interest in her. Well – except for her dad, whose close attention earned him a lengthy break in prison. In fact she was scared of men. But this was a gentle giant.

That night she drifted into sleep easily. She was holding hands with Mark as they floated across a field of buttercups. Upward she soared, Mark smiling at her, and in the field below the gesticulating figure of her mother shrank into a tiny doll. Suddenly something was wrong. Mark had let go her hand, and there he was down beside the doll – now Diana of the posters.

She awoke sweating, and lay agonising. She'd heard of 'love at first sight'. This must be it. And he seemed to like her. But competition for his affection would be red-hot. He'd never go out with her.

She also knew tales of unrequited love. Romantic and hopeful, but could be painful and tragic.

Maybe being a romantic heroine wasn't that bad. She'd keep going to the gym. Then she could see Mark. And maybe lose some weight!

Through the following three days, when she felt too stiff to return to the gym, she kept replaying her encounter with Mark. She could feel his hands touching hers as she'd lain holding the abdo cradle. Indeed in everything she did, she sensed his presence, and she'd talk to him as an imaginary companion.

Thence, at the gym daily, her confidence grew, and she extended her repertoire. When she spied Mark there, she'd stay longer. She'd catch his eye whenever she could, and delight when he'd smile back and come over to ask how she was doing. As she became and looked fitter, her resolve strengthened. She'd try to get Mark interested in her.

* * *

At the start of her final session, Mark beckoned to her. "Grace, you finish today and I go off duty soon. Come into the office a minute." She followed him. He turned to close the door behind her. What was this?

He faced her and stretched to hold her by the elbows. "You're a gutsy lass. I've been watching you. I'll miss you here, Grace. A hug?"

Eyes watering, she stepped into a bear-like embrace. After a glorious few seconds, he released her.

"Thanks for everything, Mark. You're terrific."

"You know Grace, I fancied you at school." Was he blushing? "In fact, Grace, it was right through school."

"Gosh! I'd no idea." Had she heard correctly?

"You wouldn't know. I rarely saw you, and was too shy to say. You were graceful, with a quiet beauty…" His expression changed. Thoughtful? "You don't remember, Grace. A slight little lad sitting on a bench in his first playtime at the big school. In tears. A very big boy yelling 'Tich, belt up or I'll put your head down the loo again'. You sorted that bully."

She stared. Yes, she could see the waif-like miserable figure. "I was incensed, and told the other boy never to bully you again or I'd get my big brother to beat him up." She smiled. "He backed off pronto. I guess being tall for my age helped."

Mark smiled too. "He didn't trouble me again – and neither did any other boys. Your brother must be fearsome."

"Well Mark, I'm an only child." They both laughed.

"That's when we met, Grace." He was looking serious now. "Since then you've always been and still are the only girl I'd like to walk out with."

Was she going to pass out? She leaned against the desk. "But... Diana?"

His face wrinkled and he scratched his head. "Diana?"

"Yes – well, I don't know her name. That beautiful blonde instructor I've sometimes seen around. You've hugged and kissed."

Mark suddenly relaxed in a peal of laughter. "Yes, I've feelings for her all right. But she's not attractive like you. Mary's in her twenties, married. – and," he paused, grinning, "she's my big sister."

Grace stepped in for a hug. She felt his lips seek hers. The happiest moment of her life. Surely this was love.

ENDS

18. The Golden Bird

It happened without forewarning. Hornby's secretary rang to interrupt his Birmingham meeting.

"Mr Hornby says he must see you today, Mike, immediately you're back. His office."

No night out in Birmingham then. The boss always meant what he said. "What's it about?"

"Dunno, but he said something about it being out of the ordinary."

The M1 snarl-up encouraged reflection. The boss had summoned him thus before. Last time, his nifty footwork rescued a collapsing Stuttgart deal. 'Out of the ordinary' spelt trouble. A glitch in the Italian campaign?

Whatever – trouble that would panic the boss. Trouble that he, Mike Turner, would sort. Trouble-shooting was his passion.

The adrenalin was pumping when, long after nightfall, he drove past security and into his parking space. The neighbouring Rolls confirmed the boss was indeed within the deserted-looking building. Mike sprang up the steps.

* * *

Fifty minutes later Mike stumbled out shaking and sweating, and walked mechanically and stiffly down the stairs, gripping the rail. He recalled key words 'bad news'…'recession'…'rationalise'…'Chief Exec says you must go'…'clear your desk tonight'.

He'd reacted. "A bloody sick game, Eric Hornby."

Effusively charming, legendary as the smiling assassin, Hornby masked as sympathetic. "Afraid not. I know it's hellish, Mike Turner – but there we are."

Hell, this man was serious. After unsuccessful remonstration, Mike had for the first time in his career totally lost it. Exploded. He'd thumped the desk, roared at Hornby, calling the b….r an incompetent lousy shit of a non-human being. He'd left his Judas boss sitting hunched and silent.

Mike fumbled with his room key, and locked the door after him. He charged to boot the waste-bin and heard its agony in clanging against the wall. HIS waste-bin, HIS wall, in HIS room, with HIS chair, at HIS desk!

Settling into his chair, tilting back and sipping whisky from the bottle kept in his desk drawer, he swivelled gently round 360 degrees. HIS pictures, HIS carpet.

But pounding in his head was the command 'clear your desk tonight'. Slumped over his desk, smelling and tasting through the whisky the polish applied liberally and daily, he ruminated. Maybe he'd wake up from this ghastly nightmare? Could the whole thing be a fiendish simulation – to gauge his personal stability? He half expected a knock at the door or a phone call with a reassuring explanation.

No. 'CLEAR YOUR DESK TONIGHT' was repeated with a steely seriousness Mike had never encountered in Hornby. HE – MIKE TURNER – SACKED!

He heaved at the monstrous stupidity and injustice. Why him – the up-and-coming bound for the top and nearly there?

He'd sunk himself into the Company, relishing from Junior Executive days the nickname bestowed at that early office party. "O.M., O.M.," they'd chanted, as he tried to conceal bewilderment. 'Old Man'? No – 'Organisation Man'. His dedication had been noted.

Appraisal reports had testified to his excellent track record with the Company. His experience across three continents of supervising operational activity and trouble-shooting was exceptional in breadth and balance, and his C.V. right for a multi-national top job. As Assistant to the General Manager for Europe this past half year, he knew he measured up to the latter job better than his ageing boss.

Total dedication to the Company had cost some. A marriage dead in all but legality, his beloved and formerly devoted Jenny three hundred miles away and the twins at secondary school there. Having to diet and drink carefully to regulate his stress-induced ulcer. Forsaking the golf he enjoyed and was good at. In fact, abandonment of everything but work!

Now he was sobbing. 'Clear your desk tonight!'
As grief gave way to fury, he pounded his desk with fists
then forehead. Why him – he, who had given all, had
surely proved his outstanding worth, the proverbial
golden boy?

Golden boy? Yes! He was the Golden Bird, the
high flyer whose wings had been clipped, the victim of
that game he'd noted with amusement all those years ago
in '*Management Today'*. "Kill the Golden Bird," he
yelled. "Or KGB," he muttered, smiling wryly. How
devilishly apt! He drank deeply from the bottle.

"Kill the Golden Bird," he crooned. Lethal knives
were out, with him as target. Wryly he recalled, from that
same article, the game 'Godfather', and regretted not
doing more to cultivate the acquaintance of that shit of a
yankee Chief Exec. After all he'd done! This bloody
shambles of a multi-national and its bosses. An idea came
as the whisky kept hitting his throat and he felt that
reassuring warm glow. He would set on record his utter
contempt for the top management. No way would he go
with a whimper.

Damn! His laptop was in the car boot. Ah – but Rosemary's! Striding through the connecting door to his secretary's room, he hammered out an email to Chief Exec Joe Larden, 'Mr Really Big Shit who said I must go'.

Mike sat back and admired his work. Headed 'The Golden Bird Flies Off' and marked 'Very Personal' the vitriolic text was rich in parody, spiced with expletives, and told the Chief Exec what he might do with his piddling firm. What the heck – he'd been thrown on the scrap-heap, and, at fifty, without hope of anything big elsewhere.

Pressing 'send' felt good. Staggering back to his room, he sank into his chair. His hand found the pack of paracetamols, full bar the couple he'd taken yesterday. He gulped down a couple more with a long draught of whisky. The Company was his life. And Jenny Mark and Susie with that swine, Jenny's partner! Sobbing, he looked at the remaining paras, and wished he'd bought another pack.

He jerked as the phone on his desk rang, grabbed the receiver and exhaled "uh". Through the mists he heard: "Mike Turner?"

A drawl – familiar, but from where? "Uh."

"Joe Larden, O.M."

"Eh?" Mike struggled, unbelieving. Of course, Larden had got the email. But O.M.? Had to be sarcasm. Mike didn't care. He had a chance to say exactly what he thought – if only he could coordinate his failing speech.

The hybrid of American and Welsh continued. "Hornby thought you'd still be around. You okay?"

Okay indeed. What a bloody nerve – hounding him. "'m not," Mike began, but trailed off unable to get more words out. Damn – the whisky.

"The 36-hour day?" The tone was amazingly jovial from someone feared for plain-speaking ruthlessness.

Banality and hypocrisy! "Mm – uh – you –"

"I'm fine," the C.E.O. cut in. "I'm ringing you directly because there's a crisis. I want you to take over as General Manager for Europe – from tomorrow. 'Acting' at first – we have to advertise – but I assure you, the job's yours. Okay?"

Mike couldn't comprehend. He'd been sacked, so this could not be. Maybe a wind-up – and was this really the Chief Exec? "Uh?"

"In a nutshell, Hornby must go now. On early retirement – he's near sixty – a good deal." The voice paused. "Still there, O.M.?"

"Yuh." This could be for real. But an ice-cold shaft penetrated his befuddled brain. Could Hornby have lied – and the C.E.O. not know he'd been sacked?

"I've just told him. Sounded shocked and didn't say much, but you can take it that's sorted. I've had this in mind, but you know what triggered it now? Old Hornby rang earlier to tell me about sacking you. I thought about it awhile and decided. Hornby's clearing his desk *now.*"

This was it then – the main chance. "Wheeh," he managed. But his glee was evaporating with a chilling recollection. "Th' email," he stuttered.

"Yeah, I'll confirm by email. Have a good night."

The call was over. Mike slammed down the receiver, lurched backward against the wall, toppled his chair and sprawled on the carpet – bawling aloud his frustration. Larder hadn't checked his email, but when he did..!

* * *

Stumbling out into the car park, inhalations of frosty air helped revive Mike for the short trip down the dual carriageway to his flat. He had a terrible night, wakeful, depressed and constantly replaying the evening's events. At one point he dosed off, then awoke in terror and a pool of sweat after being scorched by a giant dragon. He forced down a gallon of strong coffee, played Beethoven's Emperor Concerto repeatedly and tried to analyse his situation.

Any joy at being offered the job was obliterated by the realisation that he'd be discredited and sacked when the C.E.O. read his mail. Smith – same rank as he, with a different brief – would get the promotion instead.

He contemplated whether he could disown the message. Maybe he could pass it off as a joke? No, it would be a pretty sick one – and in any case he wasn't known for his sense of humour. He pondered how he could retrieve the situation by somehow explaining it – and tried to rehearse what he would say. No way would this work. In disgrace, he'd be sacked.

His mood was thunderous, with himself and Hornby alternating as targets. The latter gradually faded and he fixated on himself. He kept crying aloud with frustration and rage. That damned email! What an idiot – drunkard, unworthy of the human race, never mind top management. And he'd said goodbye to a decent reference. Golden Bird – huh – one spectacular failure!

* * *

7a.m., time to set out for work, came and went and he sat in an armchair, pondering. He came to a decision. HE would kill the Golden Bird – literally. The express train passed through at 8.55, and he would jump off the bridge into its path.

* * *

At 8.30 he was dressed and passing the phone, when it rang. He lifted it automatically. "Mr. Turner?" His secretary's voice. "Yes," he heard himself say.

"Thought I'd better ring to check what you want done as you're not here – just in case you're going somewhere else."

He didn't want a conversation. On the other hand, it was the last he would have. And there was plenty time to reach the bridge. "Well?"

"You sent an email to Mr. Larder after I'd gone last night."

The reckoning – so what! He felt emotionally numbed. "Yes. Look Rosemary, I'm in a hurry."

"Well – it's been returned as undeliverable. You'd missed out the full stop between 'Joe' and 'Larden'. I rang Mr. Larden's secretary to let her know what had happened."

It struck him. "You mean he hasn't had the email?"

"The secretary asked me to read it out." She coughed.

No! "Ah..."

"But I didn't like to. Said my voice was going – and that I'd tell you what had happened."

Phew! Solid loyal Rosemary. "Good."

"Shall I re-send?"

"NO. Delete the whole thing – permanently. Now, please, Rosemary!"

* * *

Mike dialled New York. Soaring above the clouds, The Golden Bird revelled in the warm sunshine.

ENDS.

19. What The Cow Thought About The Rain

To further cow-human understanding, I print this missive from Esme, Moocowland, U.K.

Bill, thank you for talking with me and asking what I think about the rain. I am pleased to hear from a human who approaches with the respect due to a fellow being and citizen of planet Earth. I understood perfectly your query and why you were asking. I hope you didn't feel slighted by my mooing in reply.

In fact I was impressed by your perseverance in listening, and attempts to interpret what I was mooing. Sadly you did not pick me up accurately. I did not say I would want to go into the cowshed (which our human despot-who-must-be-obeyed refers to as a byre). Nor did I indicate a wish for a plastic raincoat – or indeed any of the other coverings you mentioned.

You could, in contrast to the less intelligent and more insensitive humans I have encountered, see that I am anatomically challenged, in ways that mean I can neither speak nor write in your language. So I have decided to broadcast this to you ethereally, in the hope that you can connect with the extra-sensory.

What then are my thoughts about the rain? I welcome it and love it – the heavier the better! Especially in the summer, as I can sweat, even when lying on the ground in meditation. Remember, we do not have your blessing of a fitted shower to cool us. Or indeed any kind of toilet facility, which isn't a problem normally as our 'cow-pats' (a nice term for our poos incidentally) contribute a sweet and distinctive aroma. But when there's diarrhoea around, things become plain stinky.

So rain is good for our calm wellbeing and for our personal hygiene. And the grass becomes infinitely more luscious and appetising. You may have noticed that a downpour can inspire us to cluster round for a mass moo-in.

My friend, I am appreciative that you treat me as a fellow intelligent being. So often we are shouted at, herded around, even poked with a stick. And while pleased to further human survival by donating milk, I feel that an unduly tight squeeze on my udder borders on sexual abuse.

Also I deplore how we of the bovine community are portrayed in your literature. Thus the children's picture book '*The Cow that fell into the Canal*' ridicules my noble ancestor Esmeralda. Written by some misguided upstart human, this book is not at all funny, and is typical of the cow-ism so widespread among your race.

You Bill, are a rare exception. You know, the most outstanding in our cow-lore was a female human who one sunny morning, stopped to introduce herself as Elisabeth Douglas, and give our moo community in Perranporth, Cornwall a recital of 'Friends Romans, Countrymen, Lend Me Your Ears' by William Shakespeare.

All the cows in that field gathered round to lend their ears throughout, spellbound, and afterwards mooed collectively in gratitude. The lady's three small children were silent, also listening in wonder. Her boorish husband (coincidentally and most unworthily apparently named Bill), kept laughing rudely, but failed to disrupt this splendid historic event.

There are then sparks of hope for a fuller more equal understanding between our two races. But, my friend, I stray from the topic, and am in danger of moo-ranting!

I remain truly your bovine fellow spirit,

Esme.

ENDS

20. Yuppies

It's Hogmanay 1989 and I'm bored, what with Rod finishing off some paperwork and nothing decent on the telly. But I wish I hadn't said I'd want us to go for a drink at the nearest pub.

"I'll go with you, Mandy. Where is the nearest pub?"

"The Rose and Crown, Rod." It's about fifty yards along our road.

So, linking arms we go for our night out.

First shock I get comes when Rod and I go up to the bar counter of the Rose and Crown. "Well," says the barman, "haven't seen you two before. Guess you're yuppies." He gives a kind of sneering smile.

I've never heard the term, but it sounds real insulting – like 'yelping puppies' – and it does look like the guy **is** sneering.

I see Rod's bristling like he'll deck him. So I whip my arm across the back of Rod's neck like I'm cuddling in, to stop him following through on the uppercut.

I force a smile and whisper to Rod, who's struggling to get out of my cuddle. "Steady, Rod – don't want to get us banned."

The barman steps back out of reach – maybe he's read the situation. "Violet'll serve you," he says, and disappears round the corner.

We get our cocktails, and take them to a table by a window that looks out on the floodlit car park. I sit gazing at the cars and people and tell Rod what I'm seeing. But I guess he's brooding as I hear 'yuppies' now and again. "Cheers Rod, here's to us," I say, and raise my glass.

Rod starts a bit then repeats "Cheers Mandy, here's to us." We clink glasses and down our drinks.

* * *

Back at the flat, we sit at the table where Rod looks up 'yuppies' on his computer. "Young upwardly-mobile professionals," he says. "What is meant by 'upwardly-mobile, Mandy?"

"Dunno. Sounds like we climb."

"What?"

"What do you mean?"

"What do we climb?" He looks puzzled.

I feel like saying 'up a wall', 'cos I'm totally bored. But I don't, as Rod takes everything literally and would want to know what wall. "The social ladder".

"What can be social about a ladder?" he comes back with.

I know my husband is not joking. He cannot grasp subtleties, so trying to explain about a metaphor will be pooh-poohed. "I agree," I say, "that a ladder can't be social. It's just how people talk…" I'm struggling, as he wants an explanation.

"But what do they mean?" He's frowning. "If any bloke calls us yuppies, I'll punch him."

A gentle giant who means what he says. With his fists and forearms, it could be a killer blow. I must explain. "Rod, it's meant as a compliment. I –"

"Don't see how," he barks out.

We are not going to celebrate our first wedding anniversary by rowing over this stupid thing. "Well, I've figured it, Rod. I –"

"Tell me then."

I take a deep breath. "I think it means you and I look like brilliant young professional people who'll keep being promoted at work and earning more money."

I see his face muscles relax. "Now I understand," he says. "That's alright." He stands up, stretches, walks over to collapse onto the settee, and pats the space beside him. "You come here and I'll cuddle you, Mandy."

I'm no longer bored. Conversations with Rod can occasionally be a bit challenging – but they're always stimulating and good-humoured. We'll enjoy the rest of our evening, into 1990, with many a cuddle.

You know, my mathematical genius high-earning husband was, in his childhood, diagnosed autistic and now he'll say he has Asperger's. I've just volunteered to train for the local Autism Society helpline. We've been to a social and they're a friendly bunch.

I'm so lucky to be with such a wonderful talented man. We're so much in love. We both want a family – and I know he'll be a great dad.

One thing scares me a bit. While he's a real gentle fellow, if he does deck some guy like the one that called us yuppies, he could end up a guest of Her Majesty.

ENDS

Printed in Poland
by Amazon Fulfillment
Poland Sp. z o.o., Wrocław